'Sir, we need an ans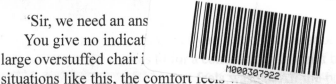

You give no indicat

large overstuffed chair i

situations like this, the comfort is supposed to make your job easier but too much stress weighs on you to enjoy.

You spin around in your chair. Your Secretaries of State, Defense, and Homeland Security stare eagerly at you, awaiting your wisdom and guidance. From their bloodshot eyes, greasy faces, and general stink, it appears they all had sleepless nights as well.

Across your desk are several high-resolution images taken by the Andromeda Satellite. They depict around two-hundred thousand pie tin shaped flying saucers on a direct course to Earth. The ships flew in triangular formations of fifty. No attempt at communication with the fleet has been responded to, so officially, no one knows the ships' intentions but you understood what you are looking at – an armada. An invasion.

Only a select few World governments with advanced space technology or spy networks are aware of this information. At the speed the ships are approaching, the whole world will know soon enough.

"Any responses so far?"

"None yet."

This is it – time to make the hard decisions. You lean back in your throne and look your advisors one by one in the eyes.

"Complex 23," you say.

The Secretary of State clears his throat and stumbles over his words, "on-n high alert and ready to act on your order."

The silence crackles with fear but you think clearly. You know what must be done.

"When will they be here?" you ask.

"The ships will reach Earth by ten-thirty hours," the Secretary of Defense says.

"What time is it now?"

"It's – "

SUPER GIANT MONSTER TIME!

Books by Jeff Burk

Shatnerquake
Super Giant Monster Time!
HomoBomb
Cripple Wolf (with Cameron Pierce)
Pothead
Shatnerquest
Bring Me the Head of Bruce Campbell
The Slaughterhouse Thrills
Sex and Death Camp
Hipster Hunter
Chrissy Must Die!
Shatnerpocalypse

CHOOSE YOUR OWN MIND-FUCK FEST

SUPER GIANT MONSTER TIME!

by Jeff Burk

Illustrated by Chrissy Horchheimer

Eraserhead Press
Portland, OR

This is a work of parody, as defined by the Fair Use Doctrine. Any similarities, without satirical intent, to copyrighted characters, or individuals living or dead, are purely coincidental.

ERASERHEAD PRESS
205 NE BRYANT
PORTLAND, OR 97211

WWW.ERASERHEADPRESS.COM

ISBN: 1-933929-96-0

Printed in the USA.

Super Giant Monster Time! is dedicated to Sophie and the Bizarro Bunker 1.0

Choose Your Character

Si A super cool punk rock chick with a massive mohawk. Fueled by alcohol and violence, she's not going to take no-motherfucking-invasion-from-beyond lying down.
Turn to page 11.

John Smithe – a boring office worker. He is afraid of: his boss, showing up late, and being the focus of attention. His favorite color is tan.
Turn to page 77.

Gary Freedman – a scientist at the mysterious Complex 23 research facility. Trapped in what was a normal super secret government facility that has now become a true Hell on Earth.
Turn to page 149.

You wake up abruptly in a tangle of blankets and pillows. Did the house just shake? You lay silent, hyper-aware of the world. In the back of your brain some primal instinct, the same that sends animals fleeing before a natural disaster, is screaming.

You wait and listen.

Nothing.

It must have been a dream. You get out of bed, feeling unnerved.

The room is a mess of clothes, books, and records. The walls are covered with posters and flyers promoting radical politics and obscure bands. You grab a pair of ripped-at-the-knees black jeans and your favorite CRASS tank top. You look at the clock; 3:00 PM. For once, you're up early.

You stumble out of your room into the dark basement apartment. Your roommates must be out.

You go into the bathroom and sit on the toilet. As you piss, you avoid looking at the black mold coating the wall next to you. You shut your eyes and try not to think of what terrible microbes you are inhaling every moment you sit there. Fucking do-nothing landlord.

A strange smell tickles your nose. It's not any one of the number of funks in the bathroom or the familiar, sweetly stinging odor of weed, crack, or meth.

It's smoke. It's fire. One of your stupid-ass roommates must have left the stove on or tried microwaving a spork again.

You wipe yourself and rush out of the bathroom, but not before sneaking a look in the mirror to make sure your Mohawk is intact. Despite the previous night's slam dancing and debauchery, it stands perfect and proud.

All is fine in the kitchen. Dishes are piled up in the sink and crumbs from previous meals blanket the counters and table. But the stove is turned off and the microwave is intact and there is no sign of a fire, although the harsh smell of smoke is even worse here. It must be coming from outside.

You have a moment of panic as you imagine the apartments above you burning. You rush to the front door and lace up your black boots.

You open the door and step out into hell.

The apartment buildings on the opposite side of the street are now a ten-story inferno. You can feel the heat of the flames from where you stand. Black smoke rolls down the street so thick that you can taste it. Through the haze, you see vague silhouettes.

You run down the street. You need to get away from this death trap.

The air is filled with screams and sirens. As you near the intersection, you feel, more than hear, a low pounding.

The next street is not much better. Random buildings are burning and the people are running in pure panic. An overturned police car is in the center of the road, its lights still flashing.

There are times in life when the whole world is turned upside-down. Moments that one can never go back from. This is yours. It's obvious that the world is ending around you.

Head further into the city to try finding safety, turn to page 153.
Go to the bar, turn to page 44.

You flick your tail angrily as you watch the mammoth squirrel rampage through the city outside your window. You lick your paw and rub the side of your head, smoothing the fur while fuming that you have not been transformed into a giant.

If anything should be remade into a massive beast of fear it is you, the divine representation of the feline species. Instead you are stuck being barely ten inches tall and at the mercy of those stupid hairless apes.

The sky outside turns a deep shade of purple and you narrow your eyes, suspicious of this new development.

You turn from the window and fly over to your food dish. You freeze right as you are about to take your first bite. Since when could you fly?

You rise into the air and hover, eager to try out your new powers. You zip through the apartment, knocking over lamps, books, and anything else not nailed down.

You land in the center of the apartment and feel many more powers surging through you. You look at the window. Red beams shoot out of your eyes and shatter the glass.

You fly outside and are high above the city.

You see a bird and rush at it. The bird is not expecting a cat to attack from above. Ten-inch razor-sharp blades come out of your paws and shred the bird in seconds. This prey falls with more ease than you would like.

You hover and look around. Your bloodlust is far from sated.

You can see the massive squirrel. That would make for a challenging target. Or what about those flying pie tins you saw earlier? They could be fun to hunt.

Attack the giant squirrel, turn to page 23.
Go flying saucer hunting, turn to page 160.

You remember a time before all this – when you were just a baby carrot growing in the ground. You would spend the day soaking up nutrients with your roots and snuggling in the warm dirt.

But then the men in white came and took you away. They were what the other carrots called *humans* – the vicious eaters of Rootkind. They took you from your home and family and experimented on you. They subjected you to blasts of radiation and forced your roots to drink stale tap water spiked with a chemical cocktail.

You grew large and strong and became more like your hated oppressors. You developed arms and legs.

You felt new things. The world of carrots knows only love and peace. You learned hate and anger.

Soon you towered over your oppressors, but they kept you locked in colossal cages to protect themselves from your wrath.

Then the flying saucers came and took you away. They made you even bigger and stronger than you were after the humans *improved* you. You were then dropped off in one of the human-populated, nature-perverting cities.

You raised your orange arms into the air and roared. The people, little black dots, fled from your magnificence.

You attacked their buildings, the monuments to their own destructive tendencies, leveling them to rubble.

You have been working on this city for a few days now. At one point the humans tried mounting a defense, but their weapons of war had no effect on your carrot-hide.

Not only have you been laying waste to buildings, you are herding the survivors like sheep to one central spot in the chaos. Soon the fires will burn everything down, leaving new fertile ground.

You can feel the beginnings of flowers in the greenery atop your body. Soon they will bloom and with them will come seeds. Then you'll put the humans to work in the new fresh fields.

Humankind will serve Rootkind

You laugh as the city burns around you, the flames clearing way for the new age of carrots.

THE END

You decide to get on the smaller ship. It looks faster than anything else around and a speedy escape is what you really value right now. It doesn't take long for the ship to get loaded up and ready to go.

The boat pulls away from the dock before most of the other ships. As you gain speed, the water starts to churn violently. Suddenly huge tentacles, as thick as tree trunks, shoot out of the water and begin tearing apart ships and scooping up people.

Your boat reaches full speed and shoots out of the dock. As you escape, you can see the large battleship becoming wrapped up by dozens of tentacles. There is the loud screaming of tearing metal and then the battleship breaks in two. It is a good thing you didn't choose to go there.

Your boat races away from the dock. You sit on the deck, lay back and quickly fall asleep.

Turn to page 34.

"At the monster," you yell and point.

The punks charge forward, chanting, "Oi! Oi! Oi!"

They swarm at the thing's tentacles as it thrashes about, crushing many attackers. Scores of people are smashed but even more take their place. The people cling to its fleshy tentacles and begin to climb. The things shakes its massive bulk, sending punks flying through the air, but it is not able to repel them all.

More punks attack and climb until the thing is people-coated up to its torso.

You turn back to the spacemen and see that they are marching steadily. Some in the front are shooting off their rifles. These space-guns shoot green beams that tear through flesh. Dozens of punks fall dead on the first volley of shots.

"Get them too!" you yell.

The punks closest to the spacemen turn and charge them. The spacemen's beams cut them down.

You turn back to the monster and see that it is now completely covered with people. The punks swarm over it like a human sheet. The thing lifts its arms but the people are just too much. It sways back and forth and then falls to the ground under the weight of the punks and their metal-studded jackets.

You turn back to the spacemen just in time to see the green beam coming at you. Your new Mohawk powers can't stop your body from being bisected at the waist. You have the strange experience of falling over but seeing your legs unmoving and standing upright.

You hit the ground and feel your insides rush onto the dirty concrete. You feel very light and hollow and then feel nothing.

THE END

After several minutes you are finally at the corner of the building and it sounds like there is a war happening just around the side. You turn the corner and that is exactly what you see.

Several dozen soldiers are scattered about, shouting and shooting at three creatures. One is a forty-foot Cyclops holding a screaming soldier in its massive clawed hands. The Cyclops tosses the solider into the air repeatedly like it is playing a game of catch. The barrage of bullets it's undergoing seem to have no effect. The creature brings the soldier to its mouth and bites him neatly in half.

Behind it is another thing, this one little more than two oak-tree-sized legs that meet at a giant eyeball. It is one of what is affectionately referred to as "the art projects." It is amusing itself by stomping on hapless soldiers until they are little more than red mash.

The third is a gargantuan slug, at least fifty feet in height. It blocks the way around the building. Its bulk starts halfway up the building's wall, goes down and across the sand clearing, into the jungle, and loops back into the clearing where it watches the battle with unnaturally human looking eyes at the ends of its antennas.

You drop your saw and staple gun. They are not going to help you here.

Closer to you than the monsters are large open hanger bay-like doors in the building. There is a large group of at least three dozen soldiers there and a set of three gun turrets, not that they are showing any signs of hurting the monsters. You begin to run to the soldiers, hoping they can provide you cover and help you. There is a high pitch squealing sound as one of those bastard flying saucers comes into view over the trees.

Two beams shoot out and hit the Cyclops and the eyeball thing. They instantly disappear.

You and all the soldiers still on the field make a mad dash for the safety of the building. The saucer opens fire and there is a series of explosions at the gun torrents. Black smoke fills your vision.

An explosion next to you sends you flying through the air. You hit the ground hard, but thankfully not hurt in any real way. You get to your knees and look around.

The doors are lost in smoke and fire but you can still hear many people yelling and gunfire through the haze. There are soldiers running past you into the smoke in the direction of the hangar doors. To your left the giant slug blocks your path to the docks. You look over your shoulder and see a group of soldiers blindly fleeing into the jungle. The saucer hovers overhead, firing at the building and those trying to escape; it is only a matter of time before it targets you.

Join the soldiers running through the smoke to get into the building, turn to page 130.

Join the soldiers fleeing into the jungle, turn to page 38.

Try to climb over the giant slug, turn to page 144.

You put the information in the computer and move on to the next form. You pause to look at the figures on the form and try to make some sense of them. Try as you might, in all the years you have worked here you have never figured out what exactly these forms are for.

You shrug and enter the information into the computer.

As you type, you notice your eyelids are getting heavy. The monotony of the work is starting to get to you and it is still early in the day. You could use some coffee for a pick up but you don't want to drink too much coffee. You've already had two cups today and if you drink too much you'll be up all night.

Wait to get coffee later, turn to page 161.
Go get some coffee, turn to page 116.

You turn and run as fast as you can. You can hear his boots pounding behind you. He is taller and faster and is going to get you – you know it.

You hit the exit door and run through. Before you is the border of sand that encircles the building. It goes out about a hundred yards and then disappears into thick tropical jungle. The air is alive with gunfire, screams, and inhuman roars. You pause, surprised to see two soldiers standing directly in front of you. They are dressed all in black and are loaded down with weaponry. They instinctually raise their rifles but relax when they see no patches, spikes, or multi-colored hair.

Before you can gush over how happy you are to see them, the door behind you opens.

"Get back," shouts one of the soldiers.

You run past the soldiers and spin around to see the punk rushing through the door. The soldiers open fire and the bullets tear him apart. The soldiers move slowly forward with their weapons raised toward the corpse.

You can hear a chorus of angry cries from the other side of the door and you cautiously back away, watching the scene unfold.

There is a piercing pain in the small of your back and your body goes limp. You are raised several feet in the air. You try to move or yell at the soldiers, but you cannot do anything.

The soldiers turn around and you can see them yelling, but your hearing seems to be gone as well. They raise their weapons as the door behind them opens and two black-clad cretins rush out. One has a chain and begins to strangle a soldier from behind. The other has a hand gun and fires off two quick shots at the other soldier, one behind each knee, followed by a third shot to the back of the head.

You are spun away from the grisly display and find yourself face to face with a scorpion the size of a tank. You are dangling from the end of its stinger.

It darts one claw forward and *SNIP* cuts off your right

leg at the knee. You can't move but thankfully you can't feel anything. Your body has gone completely numb.

The other claw moves and *SNIP* your left hand falls to the ground.

You try to scream but nothing happens. You can only watch.

The scorpion keeps doing this, *SNIP SNIP SNIP*, until there is nothing left.

THE END

You have always had a fondness for squirrel flesh so how could you resist this walking buffet. You fly down and buzz around the transformed animal's head, mewing with fury. The beast swats at you but you are too fast to be hit.

You attack the squirrel's throat, biting and slashing. You are quickly and gloriously bathed with blood. You wiggle and dig into the fur and flesh. Soon you are completely inside the thing's neck and you can feel its body convulsing. You keep tearing and soon pop out the other side.

"Mmmmeeeeeewwwwwwwwwwww!!!!!" You roar victoriously into the air while the massive corpse collapses beneath you. You fly back to the body and feast upon its flesh.

Once you have had your fill, you curl up in one of its eye sockets (now minus an eye, thanks to your desecration) and quickly fall asleep.

You flick your tail as you dream of what you will do to the hairless apes with these new powers.

You are no longer Mr. McWhiskers, you are now Mr. McWhiskers – the Super-Cat!

THE END

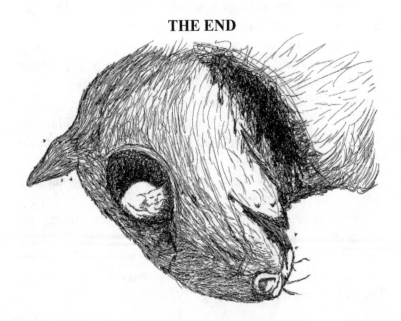

You travel ten blocks and gather another hundred soldiers before you encounter another spaceman. At your direction the punks leap upon him and tear him limb from limb. His ray gun useless and his attempts to call for help only adding to your army.

You push forward, deeper into the city.

You take notice of a low thumping sound and freeze. You don't know how long it has been there in the background. When you stop, your army stops.

You spin around and see no sign of the oncoming creature, but the pounding becomes louder and louder.

The noise brings more punks out of hiding and they join your ranks.

You spin around when another sound hits your ears. It sounds like a marching army. You know it's not yours because they are all standing peacefully and surprisingly quiet for such a large crowd of punks that has raided every commercial supply of alcohol they passed.

You can see a large group of people walking towards you in an orderly and close formation, a real army. They get closer and you see it is a ground force of spacemen. They are all armed, not with the little ray guns, but with large sliver rifles that require two hands to hold.

The pounding becomes thunder and you hear a totally unnatural roar. Approaching from the other direction is a thing at least three hundred feet tall. Its body is covered in thick brown fur and is hunched over like a gorilla. The colossal limbs of the beast end in masses of industrial cable sized pink tentacles.

Its eight eyes staring at your army with intelligence and hunger from its primate-like face.

You are trapped and you must fight. Do you direct your forces at

The oncoming spacemen army, turn to page 49.
The giant monster, turn to page 17.

Your conservative workplace appropriate haircut disappears. You sprout a huge multicolored Mohawk to replace it. Your white button up dress shirt morphs into a Leftover Crack "Kill Cops" t-shirt. You are now dressed all in black with a metal-studded leather jacket.

The world swirls around your alcohol and marijuana soaked brain.

You walk down the street kicking over trash cans and singing Clash songs.

You soon come to a bar, and being the decent and respectable street punk you are, you go inside and have a dozen drinks, get into a fight, and have sex with someone (male, female, who cares!) in the bathroom.

You are later found dead from alcohol poisoning in a piss-soaked alleyway.

THE END

You pull out spikes from your head and charge at this Trekkie firebug. He points his hands at you and great long bursts of fire shoot out. But you're too fast and you dodge the attack, the flames narrowly missing. You feel the heat on the back of your neck.

You leap at him, stabbing forward with your spikes. With a loud *CRACK* both weapons snap in half when they make contact with his chest. His uniform doesn't even tear. You both freeze for a moment, surprised.

He acts first, raising both of his hands he puts them right in your face, giving your head a double-dose of full on fire. Your vision is filled with dancing flames but it doesn't even hurt, just feels pleasantly warm.

The flames stop and you can see his cocked head regarding you. "I do not believe it is logical for us to continue this battle."

You nod, agreeing.

"Solok." He holds out his hand.

You take it and introduce yourself, "Si."

He breaks the handshake and points past you. "I believe he *is* someone it is logical to attack."

You turn around and see a lone spaceman walking towards you from across the street.

You grin and pull two fresh weapons from your head. "I got 'em."

You charge and the spaceman raises the ray gun at you and fires. You easily duck the black beam and jam both spikes into his gut. They sink in up to your hands and thick green goo oozes out from the wounds. The spaceman convulses. You pull out the blades and the corpse collapses straight to the ground.

"Piece of cake," you say while turning around.

Solok is curled up on the ground where you left him. The spaceman's raygun must have hit him when you ducked.

You rush over to him and kneel down. "Solok, are you OK?"

He is face down on the ground and coughing lightly. He lifts up his head to look at you. You gasp.

Turn to page 90.

You've seen enough already to know that Complex 23 is a lost cause. You don't really give a shit about the experiments or the work you've been doing here, not when it means you're going to die trying to save it.

Creeping down the hallway, you come to the door for the stairwell. Just down the stairs, down another hall, and then you are outside. You look around. Except for the bodies, there is no one around.

You push open the door as quietly as possible and step through. You are careful to control the door shutting behind you so as not to make a sound. The concrete stairwell has stairs leading up and down. You see no one and pause, listening intently but hearing nothing. You hold the staple gun raised and ready. You head down the flight of stairs. There is a door directly in front of you that leads to the first floor and a hallway to the right that leads outside – that's the direction you want.

BANG! You spin around as a huge punk violently slams through the door next to you. He has to be at least six feet tall with a completely shaved head but for two spikes of hair jutting out above each ear – one red, one blue. He roars and raises his fists when he sees you. In one hand is a severed arm that is still bleeding, in the other hand is a bone saw he must have gotten from one of the laboratories.

He locks murderous eyes with you and charges.

Try to make it outside before he gets you, turn to page 21.
Stand and fight, turn to page 124.

It does not take long to prepare. The supply closet, or armory as it is now referred to, is emptied for weapons. The workers arm themselves with rulers, staples, and pens. Toilet paper is duct-taped to plungers and used to make torches. You smear white-out on your face and become a twenty-first century warrior.

You all amass in the main room that contains all of the cubicles. You raise your right arm over your head and pause for a moment, savoring the smell of drying white-out. You drop your arm and the torches light at your signal. The former white collar drones now turned mighty soldiers of freedom let out a roar that would make Genghis Khan piss his pants.

The Supervisor's office door slams open and Nelson steps out, furious.

"Now what the fuck is –"

The words freeze in his throat when he sees your savage horde armed and ready for battle.

Lead a mad charge to freedom, turn to page 145.
Attack Supervisor Nelson, turn to page 88.

You leave the bar and step back out onto the street. It is plain to see that the bar is not going to shed any light on these strange events.

You can hear thunder in the distance as you walk down the street.

The thunder becomes louder and more rhythmic – there is something wrong about this. You are downtown and the skyscrapers tower around you. You spin around and look for any sign of human life, but there is no one else on the street ahead of you or behind you. In the midst of gunfire, sirens, and screams, you feel completely alone.

Three blocks ahead of you a person comes running out of an alleyway into view. The pounding becomes louder and you realize it is too rhythmic to be thunder. Next to you there is a puddle of blood on the ground from some past encounter. You see little ripple-waves radiating through the pool and that part in *Jurassic Park* when the T-Rex first attacks flashes through your head.

A colossal toddler, at least three stories tall, walks into view from the same alley where the person appeared. The giant is naked but for a diaper. It is carrying a rattler that is proportionally gigantic for the thing. Each step it takes makes the ground heave.

It shakes the rattle lazily back and forth and then, with sudden quickness, brings it down like a club on top of the running person. It slowly lifts the toy while crouching to look at the mess it made. Even from here you can see the long tendrils of viscera running from the rattler to the corpse.

You don't want to stay out in the street. You feel way too exposed here.

Duck down the alleyway to your left, turn to page 70.
Hide in the porn shop to your right, turn to page 126.

You rush forward and swing the vertebrae club with all your might. His head explodes green blood and bone. The view screen is splattered with the gore.

That was anti-climatic.

You look about the now-empty bridge thinking about what to do next. You see the empty captain's chair and can't resist sitting in it.

You sit down and lean back, placing your hands on the armrests. Suddenly, silver cords spring out of the chair around your arms, legs, waist, and neck, locking you into place. You are trapped.

You hear a mechanical whirring and feel a stabbing pain at the back of your head as the chair drills metal rods into your brain.

Then the pain is replaced with euphoria. You obtain an awareness of the saucer. It has become part of your body and you part of it. You can sense every function of the ship from life support to power.

You can even sense Mr. McWhiskers moving about inside as his killing spree takes him into the deepest bowels of the ship, hunting down any living thing aboard.

You can also access all the of the ship's data including the coordinates of the invaders originated home planet. You mentally plot the course and the saucer shoots straight out of the Earth's atmosphere at an amazing speed.

You smile as Mr. McWhiskers slaughters the last crew member. Soon you will arrive at the coordinates, the alien home world, and the two of you will bring the fight to them.

THE END

You do not need to go back and finish the fight. You have escaped from that corporate hell and with this new power there is so much more that you can do. The big picture has suddenly gotten a lot bigger.

You fly over to your apartment to save Mr. McWhiskers because if you do not, who will?

Rather than entering the front door to the building, you smash through the window.

Your apartment is in total disarray. Mr. McWhiskers flies in circles around you, mewing with joy, his long gray fur matted tightly against his small body. Whatever has changed you has also changed your cat.

He flies up to you and rubs his face against yours, purring. You hold him tight, the two of you happy to reunite in the wake of all this strangeness.

The building rocks as a monster moves somewhere close by. You can't stay here. This place is not safe. You cradle Mr. McWhiskers under your arm and fly out the window.

As you soar through the sky, Mr. McWhiskers wiggles his way out of your grip and takes flight next to you.

With this new power there is now a whole new world open to Mr. McWhiskers and you.

Go back to your office to liberate the other workers, turn to page 95.
Go after the monsters that are destroying your city, turn to page 139.
Go after the flying saucers that are responsible for all this horror, turn to page 107.

You wake up lying on your back, staring straight up at the sky. The air is fresh and the sun bright and warm. You smile, feeling at peace. You try to sit up but can't seem to get your arms or legs to work. You rock a bit on the deck and grow concerned.

Suddenly a weathered and shabby face is above you, looking down. "Holy shit! He woke up."

"I can't move," you say.

"Here, let me help you," he says and reaches down under your armpits, lifts you up with ease and sits you upright against something. That's when you can see that you are missing your arms from the shoulder down and your legs are gone at the thighs. Where they once were are now short stumps with crudely wrapped bandages.

You look up and see the deck is filled with sailors who are all very shabby and emaciated. They are all eyeing you with desire, not lust but something close.

"We have a rather large problem, you see," the man continues to speak, "we had to leave the dock without fully loading up the ship."

You look down at your stumps in horror.

"Yeah, the rendezvous point is fifteen days travel away and we only have enough fuel for a day and a half's trip. We've been stuck out at sea for twelve days now. We can't reach anyone on the radio and we never loaded on any food. So we had to improvise." He motions at you.

"You've been eating me!"

"Yeah, but you gotta look at it from our perspective. You passed out on the deck right when we left and we haven't been able to wake you up since. You were in a coma of some kind. But we've been real safe about it. We cauterized the stumps so there's no chance of infection. We didn't think you were ever going to wake up."

"I'm awake now and now I don't have any arms or legs!" You start crying.

"Now it's OK. Since you're up we can draw straws." He

looks at you and then starts laughing. "I guess that's going to be a bit hard for you. Too bad."

He pulls out a large knife and moves closer to you, his laughter drowning out your sobs.

THE END

You turn and run as fast as you can.

Two punks hunker down to meet your charge and you put your shoulder forward to barrel through them.

It's like hitting a brick wall.

You fall back to the ground, stunned, as they grab you and drag you across the ground and over to the spaceman.

You kick and punch but other punks swarm forward to restrain you, grabbing your arms and legs until you can't move at all.

The spaceman strides forward and stands by your head. It leans down over you until the black facemask is inches from your face. With a whirring sound, the visor slides up, revealing a hideous face. Its skin is red, cracked in several places. Milky pus oozes from the open wounds. It looks

more like a severe burn victim than an alien.

Its blank white eyes stare at you as the thing gasps for air. The horrible sound it makes reminds you of the time you were five and your cousin had an asthma attack in front of you.

A respirator rises up from the front of the suit and covers its mouth and nose. You can hear its breathing stabilize.

A straw-like tube juts out from the respirator and begins to make buzzing sounds. You can see tiny blades twirling around at its end.

The tube extends out and moves towards your forehead.

You shout and shake your head and body, trying to break free. More hands reach out and grab you. Three grab your head, holding you still.

You scream as the tube drills into your skull. Blood, skin, and bone bits fly through the air in front of your eyes. Your whole skull vibrates and your eyeballs vibrate in their sockets, making the whole world bounce. It breaks through your skull and your vision is still again. The world goes bright white and your limbs convulse.

The tube stops and you hear a sound like a vacuum. Your head feels lighter and lighter as the white light turns to fuzz.

THE END

You turn from the building and head for the relative safety of the jungle. The vegetation hits you like a wall of whips as vines and thorns slash at your body. You run forcing your way through the plant life.

After running God knows how long you slow down and realize that you have been screaming the whole time. You go silent and try to steady your shaking limbs.

You can hear the sound of battle in the distance but you are not sure what direction it is. You spin around but cannot see or hear any sign of the soldiers that ran out here.

You sit down to catch your breath.

The ground suddenly shifts beneath you. You stand up and see the grass you were sitting on has been replaced by jagged stones fit together like mason work. You stomp on the stones and they make an oddly hollow thump.

It clicks in your brain what you are standing on, but too late.

The colossal mouth opens and you fall through into nothingness. The teeth snap shut bathing your fall in darkness.

You keep falling and falling.

It feels likes minutes have passed and then hours. You should have hit something by now. This is impossible. The thing that swallowed you has to have an end. The creature, it can't be that big. Can it?

THE END

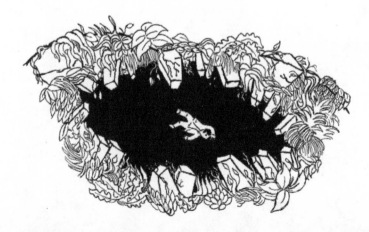

You pick the battleship. With everything that is going down you want to be near as many guns as possible. The yeoman waves you aboard and you pick a spot on the deck to watch people board and load up.

You begin to drift off in your thoughts for a minute or two when the ship starts violently rocking. You look over the edge and see the water in the dockyard brutally churning as long shapes move under the waves just beyond your vision.

Tentacles as thick as tree trunks burst out of the water. The small coast guard ship docked next to you is wrapped up and pulled underwater. Good thing you didn't decide to go there. Other ships are quickly pulled under or torn apart as dozens of tentacles attack.

Soldiers still on the docks open fire with their guns but are quickly batted away like toys by the monstrous appendages.

The battleship begins to move forward to make an escape. Tentacles reach out and latch onto the ship but it is too big and strong to hold back. You can barely contain your joy when you realize you are going to escape. The joy soon disappears as you look at the dock and see the tentacles destroying ships and massacring people.

A sailor comes up to you and asks you to go below deck as the ship heads for the rendezvous.

You are assigned a room and you head there, your body sore and tired from the day's trauma. You lie down on the bed and quickly drift off to sleep.

Turn to page 94.

You stand up and throw the stack of TPS Reports into the air and wave your arms about. And scream, "BWWWHHHAAA AHHHH PPPFFFTTTT!!!"

Everyone in the office ignores you.

Supervisor Nelson's door slams open. "SMITHE!!!"

He's a large man, at least two feet taller than you and twice as broad.

You sink back into your chair and look out the window. The creature is now dancing a jig, playfully tossing its claws over its head and jumping back and forth. Each move toppling buildings and surely destroying thousands of lives.

Nelson is now towering over you. You shrink smaller into your chair.

"Now what the fuck is the problem," Nelson screams in your face. He had tuna fish for lunch.

You turn and point to the creature, which is now humping the courthouse.

Nelson looks out the window and straight at the thing.

"I don't see nothing," he says.

"But, but –"

Nelson cuts you off, "I don't see nothing! Now get back to work!"

He storms back to his office and slams the door.

Out the window, the creature is still frantically thrusting against the courthouse, its actions a flagrant disregard for law and order. It faces you and rises one claw. It looks like it is waving at you.

Not sure what exactly to do, you wave back.

You sit back in your chair and consider the situation.

Try sneaking out of the office , turn to page 112.
Organize an employee uprising against Nelson, turn to page 102.
Get back to work. Those TPS Reports aren't going to take care of themselves, turn to page 97.

You don't want to fight the helicopters, they are humans just like you are...used to be. But you don't see any other choice.

You wait until the helicopters are close but not close enough to attack you. You open your mouth and, just like before, a bright blue beam shoots out and tears into the helicopters. In an instant all the helicopters are nothing more than brightly burning wreckage hurtling to the ground.

As you watch the burning metal plummet, something strange happens to you. You don't feel bad for what you did. You like it.

You turn to a nearby building and slam your body into it. The structure collapses to the ground sending up a cloud of dust from the rubble.

You turn your head and see a crowd of humans running away. You open your mouth and your beam burns them all to a crisp.

You raise your head high into the air and roar. You stomp down the street knocking over buildings and burning fleeing crowds of people. You finally understand why monsters do this.

This is going to be fun.

THE END

The thing's claws grab onto two other screaming workers as you run toward the beast's face. It is looking through one of the holes that it is bashing into the side of the building.

You are at the edge and look around for something to use as a weapon to fend off the monster – your supply closet arms will not do. The thing is crunching on another white collar snack. You only have moments before its attack will resume.

You are still looking about frantically when a desk comes flying through the air and slams into you, sending you sliding toward the open air and a fifty story fall. Your head spins and you look up to see Nelson running at you with a filing cabinet raised above his head.

You get to your knees but he's already on top of you, slamming the cabinet down into your face. You fall back, blood pouring from your mouth, nose, and ears, and your arms flail out into open air.

Nelson stands above you and gives you a swift kick in the balls, causing immense pain and humiliation. He pushes you further over the edge.

Your head falls back and you see the monster eyes twitching with hunger lust at you two. It has finished its snack and is ready for more.

You try to warn Nelson of the immediate danger, but another kick to your bruised and busted balls silences you.

The claws snatch up you and Nelson. You both struggle but the grip is steel-strong. "This is all your fault," screams Nelson.

You son of a bitch, you think as you get popped into the monster's mouth. The teeth come grinding down and the world goes black.

THE END

If this is the end you're not going out sober. At a time like this there is only one option: The Rat's Nest, a dirty little hole in the wall with a jukebox filled with street punk, hardcore, anarcho, and some dub reggae.

The bar is only five blocks walk away. You see more fires and fleeing people on your way but nothing that hints at the cause of all this. You try to stop one woman as she runs by but when she gets a look at you she only screams louder runs away.

You get to the bar. Thank God it hasn't burned up yet. You just hope they're open.

You open the door and find the place packed. It is wall-to-wall dreadlocks, Mohawks, and shaved heads. Everyone must have had the same idea. Aus Rotten is blaring and the air seems to be nothing but weed and cigarette smoke. You can't even smell the fires in here.

You push and shove your way through the crowd to get to the bar. A cute guy with rainbow liberty spikes dressed in all black is tending. You make eye contact and open your mouth to order. He smiles and places a full bottle of whiskey in front of you before moving on to the next customer.

You take the bottle. Must be an "end of the world" special.

You work your way into the crowd and try talking to people to find out what is going on. Everyone ignores you. You stand directly in front of some kid who looks twelve. He's wearing a Casualties shirt and already so drunk he can't stand steady. You scream, trying to get over the music, but he pays you absolutely no mind.

You chug, frustrated.

The song ends and the bar falls eerily silent. It dawns on you that there has been no conversation since you've entered; the music was just covering up the silence. You feel the same sense of doom you felt when you first woke up.

Smash the nearest person in the head, turn to page 159.
Leave to get answers somewhere else, turn to page 30.

You take one of the red vials from the cabinet. You hold it up to your eyes to inspect it. The liquid is cloudy and swirling, like thick beer.

You drink it all in one gulp. It tastes like those fireball candies.

You don't feel anything right away and wonder how long it will be before it takes effect.

You suddenly realize that you are pacing back and forth. You stop yourself and try to calm down. You tell yourself there is nothing to be nervous about.

You then feel intense heat inside yourself. It feels like the very air around you is beginning to boil. You begin to claw at your clothes. You need to get them off. It is just too hot.

The air gets hotter and hotter and you collapse to the ground, gasping to breathe through the suffocating heat.

And then, with a *POP*, your body explodes. The room is neatly coated with fine layers of gore and, where you fell to the ground, there is a smoldering, human-shaped black burn.

What an interesting weapon for chemical warfare. Imagine the possibilities of turning your enemies into unwitting suicide bombs. Too bad this didn't help you.

THE END

You watch what's left of the White House smolder on the view screen.

You look back at Mr. McWhiskers. His head is cocked sideways looking at you, "Oi?"

You smile, "Where next?"

"Oi!"

He hits a few buttons and the ship takes off to a new target.

You walk around the bridge, stepping over bodies and eyeballing your bizarre pet. The music gets louder and Mr. McWhiskers starts thrashing about on the control panel – creating a one-cat mosh pit.

You smile and go over to the captain's chair and sit down to relax. Once your body touches the chair, the music cuts out and loud sirens start going off. Red lights flash on the bridge while dozens of thin metal wires shoot out of the chair and wrap around you. You struggle but the wires have you bound to the chair.

"Mr. McWhiskers, help!"

But Mr. McWhiskers is undergoing a similar struggle. Dozens of wires have him pressed flat against the control panel, "Oi…"

The wires get tighter and tighter and start to break your skin, thin lines of blood spreading out all over your body. You scream. They sink painfully slow into your flesh. One wire is wrapped around your head, across the bridge of your nose. When it gets to your eyes, the world goes black with pain. You can feel fluid from your mangled eyes running down your cheeks.

Mr. McWhiskers howls behind you.

The wires shoot straight through you, and your body flops down around the captain's chair in dozens of wet lumps.

THE END

You look over your delirious acolytes and give them your first and final decree, "You are all now free!"

The people cheer and go rushing out of the office place without even bothering to gather their personal possessions.

You are left alone with Supervisor Nelson's corpse and Mr. McWhiskers.

"You know what, Mr. McWhiskers? I think everything is going to be OK from now on."

He starts cleaning the blood off his paws.

"Come on," you start toward the door, "let's go home."

Mr. McWhiskers glares but then follows you out. You two take the elevator down the building's lobby.

"I'm so proud of us and all that we accomplished today."

Mr. McWhiskers purrs.

The elevator reaches the lobby and the two of you exit. You freeze when you see what is happening on the other side of the lobby's doors. The entire staff of the office is being massacred by a group of giant ants. The things are tearing everyone limb from limb and then feasting on the hunks of flesh they tear off. People are running and screaming, trying to get free, but the ants have the workers surrounded and there is no escape. One person is vainly spraying a can of bug spray.

You turn to Mr. McWhiskers, "Oh yeah, the giant monsters."

Mr. McWhiskers responds with a "Rrooar?"

Before the guard abandoned the front desk he forgot to turn the television off and a cheesy laugh track fills the lobby.

THE END

You turn away from the beast. You need to keep your focus.

You point and yell, "Attack the spacemen!"

The punks scream as one and charge at the alien invaders.

The aliens let loose with their rifles. Instead of the black beams, green beams burst forth and tear into the charging mass. The beams neatly cut through limbs and torsos – sending arm, legs, and heads flying through the air.

But too many are charging. The punks attack en mass and as one. Their invader's guns may equal instant death but there are just too many people.

The punks slash with knives and bash with bats. The aliens' bodies, not used to Earth's atmosphere and not at all agile, fall quickly beneath their attackers.

You charge with your army.

You stab forward with the spikes, tearing spacesuits and breaking helmets, exposing fragile bodies to the deadly atmosphere.

You look back and the monster is still coming closer, tearing through buildings, punks, and spacemen alike.

Your forces break the spacemen's lines and you all keep charging forward. Ahead you can see several saucer ships on the ground. There are some spacemen standing guard but they are quickly overrun and torn down by the punks.

The ground shakes even harder, nearly throwing you off your feet. The monster is almost on top of you.

Lead an assault onto the saucers, turn to page 134.
Attack the monster, turn to page 115.

You sprout thick black rimmed glasses. Your hair turns into a stylish black-dyed asymmetrical do. Your black dress pants turn khaki and your button up dress shirt grows an argyle sweater vest over top.

You are overcome with the sadness of this world and your fate. You crumble to the ground crying.

The spaceman cocks his head at you, then becomes disinterested and moves on.

Why, oh why, are you cursed with this feeble existence? You know you could be so much more. If only your family was more supportive…if only you had a girlfriend…things could be so much better.

The sorrow of it all is crippling. You kick a trashcan and twist your ankle.

It will be OK, you know. You will go home and listen to Saves the Day and you will be connected to others who comprehend this kind of loneliness.

Then you get stepped on by a giant walking carrot.

Serves you right you piece of shit.

THE END

Night comes and then morning and with the new day the demon returns. It rises majestically and horribly out of the water. It regards the lifeboat with cruel, intelligent eyes and reaches forward, picking up a sailor. The demon lifts the man high in the air and then drops him in its mouth. He chews and you can hear breaking bones and death screams.

The monster disappears underwater once again.

The same thing happens the next day.

And the day after that.

You are now alone and have been on the boat for three days. You consider killing yourself before the demon comes back but you have nothing and there is nothing on the boat that would work. You could go into the water and take a couple deep breaths but you can't bring yourself to enter the waves – that's where the demon is, somewhere.

It is night but you will not be sleeping. You know what tomorrow will bring and all you can do is wait.

THE END

You've heard too many weird things about Farnsworth to follow him into a secret passageway. He motions to you to follow with his hand and you shake your head. You start toward the Control Room.

"Have it your way," Farnsworth says. He retreats in the passageway and shuts the door. There is no sign he was ever even there.

You move slow and silent to the Control Room door. You press your ear to the door but hear nothing. You push it open and walk in.

The room is pitch black. Even with the lights out, the room should be bathed in the cool blue of computer screens.

The door slams shut behind you, cutting off the little bit of light that was leaking in.

You spin around in the dark trying to get your bearings. A pair of hands grabs your shoulders from behind and pulls you back. You stumble and fall. Another set of hands grabs your feet and hoists you into the air.

You are slammed down on a table and a bright light flashes on directly above your face. It is blinding. You squint and look around. There is a fat shirtless skinhead holding your feet down and another holding down your arms. They tie your limbs to the table legs.

Two people spring up on your left and right. One is a woman with two bright blue spikes on each side of her head, twisting up like horns. The other is a man with a green Mohawk and a surgical mask covering his face. They are both dressed all in black.

"He is unchanged," says the man wearing the surgical mask, "immediate surgery is required."

He raises his hand and you see he is holding a scalpel. The skinhead above you grabs your head.

The man starts slicing along your hair line on each side of your head. The blade digs in hard and you can feel it scrape bone. You scream as your blood soaks the table.

The man stops. "I can't work under these conditions.

Nurse, please apply piercings."

The woman grabs your mouth and purses your lips. She drives a pen through your lips and leaves it. Binding your mouth and spraying your face with a red mist. She pushes another through and another. When she is done there are five pens through your lips. It hurts too bad to even try screaming.

The man goes back to work. He digs his fingers into the cuts and grips the flaps of flesh just above your ears. He pulls back hard, tearing your scalp away from your head. He continues until the skin is only attached to your head by a strip down the center.

"Stapler," he says.

The woman hands him a plain office stapler. He uses it to attach both the opposite sides of your scalp together.

He stands back and smiles, admiring your wonderful new Mohawk.

THE END

You always knew you were going to die at your job, just not like this. It's not like you were one of those extremely dedicated employees that wouldn't leave his desk even for a heart attack.

No, you just knew that you would never make enough money working as a low level security guard to retire. You knew you were doomed to a life of low wages and a dishonorable death.

But you had no idea it would be anything like this.

The gargantuan penis above you is now moving even faster and quicker.

You are locked in the vault of the courthouse. It seemed like the safest place when the monster started attacking. You think you are going to be OK until a several-foot-wide hole breaks open in the ceiling.

For a brief moment you see clear calm blue sky but then an angry red eye fills the hole. It pulls away and you fear the creature will tear off the roof and reach in for a snack. Instead the thing inserts its cock, which is at least fifteen feet long, into the hole, and starts pumping away.

You watch in horror as the massive organ moves in and out. The movements stop and the colossal cock begins to quiver.

Oh shit, you know where this is going.

Semen bursts out and the slimy white spray slams into you, knocking you to the floor. You scramble to your feet and out of the way. Long white tendrils of cum stretch from you to the floor. It flows into the room, flooding up to your knees, before the cock stops spraying.

You hold your breath and look up, wondering what will happen next. Then the semen starts flowing again. Cum rises past your waist, past your shoulders, and you have to start swimming in the thick goo.

Finally, the thing's seed stops flowing. The creature's cock is no longer erect. It is now a third of the size and hanging limply.

Oh, thank God, you think as you tread "water" and try not to swallow any of the thick milky liquid, *it's finally spent.*

You wait for the flaccid member to withdraw from the hole so you can paddle over and make your escape. But the thing does not pull out.

It starts to piss. The hot urine mixes with the cum and the liquid level begins to rise again.

The last few inches of air disappear and you are completely submerged. You know you don't want to try to breathe. You hold your breath and clamp your stinging eyes shut. You wish you could pass out. But you gasp anyway and monster semen/urine fills your lungs.

You sink slowly down into the white-yellow sea.

THE END

You would love to land and get these weak creatures' blood on your hands, but the ground is still a battlefield and you didn't become a great general by taking unnecessary risks. That's for the grunts.

You order the navigator to hold a steady course and direct the weapons operator to open fire. It does not take long to clear all human life from the area.

You are still in your ship when you are notified that humanity is extinct. You feel a bit of sadness at hearing this. You were hoping for a chance to cause much more devastation.

Oh well, now it's time for the victory ceremony. You don't enjoy the pomp and circumstance but you understand the need for it all. Ritual and tradition are useful tools for keeping the troops in line.

The ships land at the victory location. You exit the ship. Your cheering army surrounds you. They have erected a massive mountain of skulls, which you climb. The brittle bones break beneath your feet as you ascend. At the top is a throne, also made of skulls.

You sit on your ivory perch and stare out at thousands of joyous warriors who praise your name.

Today is a good day.

THE END

You walk down the hall clutching the staple gun, but you know with the experiments on the loose, the weapon will be no help.

Hall after hall you journey through until, finally, you make it to the one that leads to the control room. You look down at the door, almost unwilling to believe you actually made it this far.

The door to the control room opens and one of those spacemen walks out. It raises its raygun and fires at you. You duck to the left and narrowly avoid the black beam. The spaceman takes a few steps forward, aims, and fires again. Once again you manage to dodge the blast. This lucky streak can't keep up.

The spaceman is now ten feet from you. He raises the gun. You know he will not miss this time and you do not have the strength to attack and overpower him.

A door slides open in the wall next to the spaceman where there should not be one. The spaceman does not notice the hand with the gun reaching out from the passageway. The weapon is level with the visor on the spaceman's helmet. The gun fires and the visor shatters away.

The creature within the helmet has a vaguely human face but looks like a severe burn victim. The thing opens its mouth but no sound comes out. Its eyes are bulging out of their sockets and then with a *POP*, the spaceman's head explodes, splattering thick, creamy green goo across the walls and floor.

The holder of the gun steps from the secret doorway. It's Alfred P. Farnsworth, the super-secret scientist who was supposedly in charge of the whole facility. No one you know has ever actually met him. Many even speculated that he was not even real, the he was a figment of the government's overactive imagination.

His wall-sized portrait decorates the cafeteria, so you recognize his round squat body, pig nose, crew cut, and coke-bottle glasses.

"Come, follow me," he says, motioning toward the hallway he just appeared from.

You look at him and then at the door to the control room, it is just a few meters away.

He sees you looking at it, "Don't bother, the control room has been completely compromised."

Follow Farnsworth into the hidden passage, turn to page 92.
Go to the Control Room to regain control of Complex, turn to page 52.

You open your eyes deep underwater. There is almost no light but that does not impede your progress. Your limbs push you smoothly through the water and you can feel a large shell protecting your body.

You look around and see that you are in the middle of a group of dozens of creatures, all just like you. They look like turtles, except most turtles don't have large tusks jutting from their mouths.

The school of monsters is swimming lazily through the water. You decide to rise to the surface to see where you are.

As you begin to go up, the rest of the beasts follow you. You break the surface and look around. You are off the shore of a big city. The flying saucers circling it and smoke rising from a dozen different locations ensures that is where you will find a fight.

You swim toward shore and all the other monsters follow. You and your army hit land and you are surprised to find that you are able to walk on just your back legs – turtles shouldn't be able to do that.

A group of flying saucers is parked nearby on the sand and you rush toward them. You are about three times as big as the saucers, so when your body slams into the closest one it flips several times in the air before crashing and crumpling like a tin can.

When the other monsters see you do this, they begin to attack the other flying saucers.

Wow, you think, *that was easy*. It took you no time to build a monster army.

You join the attack on the saucers. Now the spacemen are beginning to organize and fight back. A beam from one of their rayguns cuts right through your shell. You cry out as green blood splatters on the sand.

All the other turtles stop their attack and turn to look at you. You can see slobber dripping from their mouths and hunger in their eyes. They all ignore the spacemen and charge at you, mouths and teeth gnashing.

You think, *but turtles aren't cannibals!* And then they fall upon you.

THE END

You come to in utter darkness. You try to move your body but there is tremendous pressure all over you and you can't budge at all.

What happens comes flooding back to you and you realize that you are beneath what used to the building you were thrown into. Your super-strength protected you from being crushed to death but now you find yourself stuck.

You scream for help.

Turn to page 137.

The poor fools.

Your tentacles dart down, snatching up members of the crowd and shoving them into your mouth. Your teeth grind them into a fine pulp, your meal's screams and bone-cracking are a sweet song to you. Your followers don't agree. They scurry away in terror.

You climb onto land and start smashing their monuments to stupidity.

Above you, the sky turns from light blue to deep scarlet.

Every living thing across the planet hears a chorus of unearthly cries and the world goes insane. In Japan, sushi rolls force their way down diners' throats, choking them to death. In Mexico, prairie dogs attack towns en masse, using the moment as their opportunity for revenge against their cruel human oppressors. In Iran, a small boy is beaten to death by a pack of living prosthetic limbs.

You were the first to awaken but you are not the last.

A new eon has come to Earth.

THE END

The coin comes up tails so you go right. You slosh over to the door. Mr. McWhiskers flies behind you, careful not to get his paws wet.

The door has a big red button next to it on the wall. You push the button and the door slides open, like something out of *Star Trek*. Maybe that poster does make sense.

You step into blackness. You move forward with your hands outstretched. Mr. McWhiskers hisses behind you.

The door slides shut, cutting off what little light there was. You stumble forward and hit a spongy wall. You back away from it into another wall. You reach out and find that there are now walls on every side of you.

Suddenly, bright lights illuminate the room.

There does not appear to be any kind of wall around you. You are standing in the center of the open room, but when you try to move in any direction you hit an invisible blockade. Mr. McWhiskers mews angrily next to you. He is contained in a similar trap.

There are spaceman with ray guns point at you two. The aliens are making a strange, rhythmic, screeching noise.

They take both of you to an intergalactic zoo and place you in an exhibit with another man. He has become unhinged at being taken captive by aliens that he rants and raves all day and night about being "unstuck in time," whatever that means.

Eventually, Mr. McWhiskers becomes so annoyed with the fellow that the cat slits his throat and rolls around in the man's blood.

THE END

You run to the cabinet and in a moment of insanity-induced brilliance, you down all the vials of blue liquid. You use your sleeve to wipe the stuff from your lips and turn around. Just like before, you feel nothing new or different.

You stare at the chair you were just sitting in and concentrate. Suddenly, the chair lifts into the air, flies across the room, and smashes into the far wall.

Holy shit, it worked.

You turn and face the cabinets. You raise your hands to your temples and concentrate as hard as you can. The whole wall in front of you bursts and crumbles to the ground. You are overlooking open jungle from three stories up. You walk along the ledge and survey the scenes of war before you.

Flying saucers are soaring through the air and monsters roam free, attacking soldiers armed with machine guns. The air is thick with the stench of smoke and death.

But now you can change it all.

You decide to take out the flying saucers first. You place your hands to your temples just like before and concentrate on all the saucers at once. Your whole body shakes as you charge your psychic attack.

You hear a sound like boiling water, but it's coming from inside your own skull, and then you collapse to the ground – dead even before your knees buckle. Your brain, now hot steaming muck, leaks out of your nostrils. On a countertop nearby, a spoon bends.

That was pretty fucked up.

THE END

You never thought it would come to this, you see no choice but to use the secret super weapon. You walk the half mile from your shack to the secret clearing. You stand on a hill overlooking the large football-field-size area of grass. You pull the remote control from the secret pocket of your hunting vest.

You push the button on the controller and the grass plane flips open to expose two giant metal doors. White steam billows out from the revealed chasm and a metal platform rises up and locks into place.

In the center of the platform are a steel box and an altar with a dagger and an old book on it.

That accursed book.

You pick up the dagger and open the book. You begin to read the spell. You hoped this day would never come, but you would rather give this planet to its original owners than these invading alien scumbags.

Directly above you a vortex breaks open in the air. It looks like a mini black hole. It spins around and you can hear unearthly chanting from somewhere deep inside it.

You flip open the lid of the metal box and freeze in horror. The baby is dead. You reach inside and pull the corpse out. Gripping it firmly by one foot, you hold it out in front of you. The body is blue and bloated. It has been dead for some time. You see the food and water you left is untouched. The damn bastard just up and died.

You toss the body aside. The ground shakes from the monster's roar as it gets closer.

You need a sacrifice for the spell to work. You look around in desperation but there is nothing useable. You grip the dagger tighter. Once the spell has been started, you can't stop. You can only see one option and you don't like it.

You speak the next lines from the book and raise both your hands into the air; one is holding the dagger, the other is open with fingers outstretched.

In one quick motion you drag the blade across your wrist.

Blood flows out and travels through the air into the swirling void above you.

You begin feeling weak as the blood drains from your body. It's difficult, but you manage to get out the last words of the spell before you fall dead.

In the sky, new stars blink to life and somewhere on Earth, the beast wakes.

THE END

You look at all the people bowing down before you and it feels so right. Their devotion, their praise, touches a part of you inside that has never been reached before.

"Everyone listen up!"

They all turn their heads at you.

"Get back to work! Those TPS Reports won't fill out themselves."

The workers look at each other, unsure of what exactly to do. They weren't expecting this from you.

"Mr. McWhiskers."

He nods at you and then flies at the nearest worker. It's Johnson from accounting. Mr. McWhiskers tears out his throat. Before his corpse hits the ground, Mr. McWhiskers has already torn out his eyes, tongue, and genitals.

The other employees, having seen this, rush as quickly as possible back to their desks. Within seconds they are all totally immersed in their work, as if the brutal coup d'etat had never taken place.

You return to the Supervisor's office and walk in. The windowless walls lack decoration. Everything is painted black. The file cabinets, desk, and very cushy looking chair – all black. The monochrome room is a vacuum, absorbing all light.

Mr. McWhiskers pokes his head through the door as you sit behind the desk and prop up your feet.

"Mr. McWhiskers, could you bring me a cup of coffee?"

He scurries off and the door shuts behind him, bathing you in total beautiful darkness.

THE END

You say the first thing that comes to mind.

"Bow down and worship me!"

They all stare at you in silence and then at each other. To your surprise, the crowd drops to their knees and bows before you. They hold their arms above their heads and wave up and down at you, like you are their personal Mecca.

"My people, to your feet," you yell.

They stand.

"It is time we take back this planet. This is our world. Now we take the battle to them!"

They cheer.

You push your way through the crowd and lead your army onwards

Turn to page 24.

You see an alleyway to your left and duck down it just as the giant baby turns in your direction. It wobbles forward awkwardly. You can hear and feel the pounding of its massive feet as you run. You just pray that it is not coming for you.

You are about a hundred yards into the alley when the baby steps into view. You look over your shoulder in horror, but it hobbles past.

Thank God.

You continue through the alley until you come to the next street. You peer out but see no signs of any giant things.

You walk down the street with no particular destination in mind. As you go on, you take notice that not only are there no monsters on the street to torment you, there is nothing on the streets. No people anywhere. Just the close sounds of a happening war.

You go down several blocks and still come upon no sign of anybody. You are just beginning to get really freaked out when you see a figure in the distance coming towards you.

"Hello," you yell and run towards it.

You stop half a block away.

A person in a white full-body spacesuit is walking towards you, wearing a helmet with a black tinted visor that prevents you from seeing who is within.

You stare silently, not sure what to do.

The spaceman continues walking, then stops about ten feet from you. He raises a hand and that's when you see the raygun he is holding. You try to dodge out of the way but you are too late.

The gun emits a black beam that hits you dead-center in the chest. You expect to feel pain or be hurled to the ground but nothing happens.

The spaceman cocks his head at you, confused, and fires again. Yet nothing happens to you.

You hold out your arms and look over your body but see no sign of injury.

You now feel angry for getting so worried over the beam.

"Hey," you say, stepping within a foot of the spaceman, "what's the big fucking idea?"

He ignores you and starts pushing buttons on the front of his spacesuit.

You are ready to punch him in his stupid helmet when you get the feeling you two are no longer alone.

You look around and see at least fifty punks. Most are holding weapons of some kind. All are staring at you with murder in their eyes.

You are completely surrounded.

Make a run for it, turn to page 36.
Stand your ground and fight, turn to page 136.

You run, panting and wheezing through the street. In your mind you always like to think of yourself like the super-villain The Kingpin, but the truth of the matter is you are closer to John Goodman. Your considerable bulk may give you force but it does not give you speed.

A gang of five weapon-wielding skinheads chases you.

Every part of your body is in pain. You hear the steel-toed boots quickly gaining. The sky above is now a deep violet. Your brain must already be shutting down. You may be lucky enough to black out before the skinheads get really nasty.

A lead pipe slams into your back and drives you to the ground. The gang circles you and beats you with bats and pipes. You curl up and try to protect your head. You are being pummeled but you feel no pain.

They continue striking and you still don't feel anything. You uncover your head and immediately an aluminum baseball bat slams into your face.

You feel nothing. You look down at your body. There are no wounds and no blood.

You smile and stand up. The punks keep at you, but they cannot even scratch you.

You grab the closest punk by the head, one massive hand on each side, and squeeze. His body starts to convulse and his skin flushes deep purple. His eyes pop out and dangle from their optic nerves. Blood flows freely from the sockets, his nose, and mouth. You can hear a sound like snapping wood as his skull gives way. Your hands suddenly meet each other, spraying a shower of blood, brain matter, and skull fragments.

The other punks back away from you. Their weapons are still raised. This fight is not over yet.

You turn around, shaking the viscera off your hands. You smile at your combatants.

This is going to be fun.

THE END

You sit up a little higher in your chair so you can look over your computer. You glare at John Smithe.

You don't like him.

You could tell from his first day, 1,019 work days ago, that he was a worthless employee. He doesn't take the work seriously, it takes him too long to complete an assignment, and you bet he doesn't even know what the TPS Reports are for.

And now, you look down at the note he handed you a moment ago. He is planning a mutiny against Supervisor Nelson. Of all the nerve!

At 11:14, he drops his pen and goes back to the break room. Amazingly, everyone in the office stands and follows.

You duck down in your cubical and wait for the traitors to pass by. You get on all fours and peek around the wall. You watch John hype the drones up with his blasphemous message. The hoard raids the supply closet, adding theft to their already sizable list of charges.

You crawl out of your cubical and make your way to the Supervisor's office. Outside his door, you sneak a quick look back. The mob is still distracted.

You know you should knock, but the noise might alert the others to your plan. So as quickly and quietly as possible, you open the door, rush in, and shut it behind you. You turn around but instead of Supervisor Nelson, you are greeted by a Tyrannosaurus Rex with a head the size of a jumbo jet. The outer wall of the office has been demolished and you stand on a ledge fifty stories high. The beast eyes you as drool and fragments of wood and concrete fall from its open mouth.

This is impossible. You know that dinosaurs aren't real and that God planted fossils six thousand years ago as a test of faith.

The monster's head darts forward with speed that seems unnatural for a beast of such large size.

It takes a bite and proves you wrong.

THE END

You decide to head deeper into the complex. Too many people, including you, have dedicated too many years of their lives to this project. Not to mention that if the experiments have gotten loose, it will not matter if you escape. The whole world will be doomed.

Holding out your staple gun, you creep down the hallways. The control room is three floors up and on the opposite side of the immense building. You don't know how you are going to get there alive but you have to risk it.

You creep your way up three flights of stairs poised and ready to fight the whole time, each step echoing too loudly for your comfort.

You make it to the third floor and go through the door. One of the complex's maintenance workers is crucified to the wall with nails. Two additional nails stab through the worker's eyes.

You lean over and throw up. In between painful heaves you hear a wet slithering sound. You force yourself upright and hold out the staple gun, resisting the rolling waves of nausea.

The shitty stapler does not seem so comforting anymore.

There are two directions ahead. If you go left, you will come to the control room. There is your best chance at regaining control of the facilities. If you go right, you will come to the laboratories. There's your best chance at getting some better weapons to protect yourself.

Go left in the direction of the control room , turn to page 58.
Go right in the direction of the labs, turn to page 156.

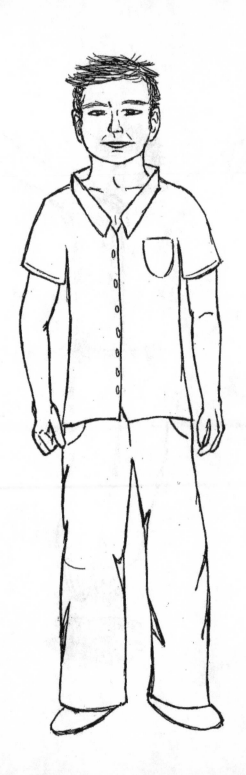

You started off your day at the office just like any other. You had a stack of TPS Reports that had to be completed by five and six databases that needed to be updated with customer information on three hundred new clients.

When the reports came in of aliens attacking and giant monsters rampaging, Supervisor Nelson came out and gave an announcement to the office promising immediate termination and sodomy if anyone left early. To quote; "I don't wanna hear no goddamn motherfucking bullshit about 'concern for loved ones' (he said this part in a high pitch girly voice). If anyone so much as thinks of leaving early, I'll bend you over your desk and fuck you in the ass myself. We have deadlines to make, people. Those TPS reports aren't going to file themselves!"

So you after that you did the same as everyone else in your workplace, you stayed and worked.

You take another TPS Report and place it in front of you. The paper has become a mess of nonsensical numbers and letters to you. Any meaning it once had is lost.

You sigh and look around. Everyone else seems to be working hard. There are about fifty small cubicles in your office. The walls are corporate white and are decorated with inspirational posters. Your favorite is the kitten hanging from the tree branch. "Hang in there." It always makes you giggle

In the back corner is Supervisor Nelson's office. He's the only one deemed worthy of having a door. On the opposite side is the break room, supply closet, and bathroom.

At least your cubicle is next to the windows. You lose yourself looking out over the city.

Wait – is that smoke you see in the Abandoned Warehouse District?

You squint your eyes. You can see smoke and fire. A black curtain rises up, blocking your view.

You look around to see if anyone else is noticing this but everyone is working.

You turn back to the window and watch the fire and

smoke. A gust of wind parts the haze.

This reveals a thing amongst the buildings. Its segmented body rises high into the air, dwarfing everything around it, and it lifts two massive claws over its head. On its head are two long twitching feelers. It shakes and roars so loud the entire office vibrates.

The creature, now facing your office building. You know it is impossible but you would swear that its beady eyes are looking straight at you. The beast lumbers forward in your direction.

You are the only one who has taken notice of the monster. Everyone else is still working intently.

Stand up, wave your arms, and scream for everyone to flee and save themselves, turn to page 40.

Sneak out of the office to make a run for it, turn to page 112.

You come to, tied down and spread-eagle on a table in the center of a room. You move your pounding head around and see that you are still in the porn shop. The woman and the pig are gone and now you are center stage.

You feel cold and realize that you have been stripped of your clothes. Next to you a bright light turns on, hurting your eyes. You hear the electrical whine of a machine turning on and you realize you are being filmed.

"I just talked with Vinchetti. He's real happy to be gettin' a two-for' on this shot," says a voice in the darkness.

You can feel and hear the sounds of something large approaching you. Not as large as the things outside, but too big for a human.

You strain your neck and see the thing walking into the light.

Its football-shaped head almost touches the ceiling. Grapefruit-sized eyes gleam lustfully at you. A tongue like a large gray slug runs across broken teeth and bleeding lips.

Worse than its terrible face is its naked body. Its skin is cracked, boil-covered, and bleeding all over. Between its legs is a cock the size of a fire hydrant. You can't call it a dick because it doesn't resemble any dick you've ever seen. It is bloated from sores, infection, and warts. The slit at the tip isn't even visible from the steady stream of puss.

You hear the man from behind the camera, "We're going to need more lube to get this started." The other men laugh

You scream and the thing moves for you and the building begins to shake rhythmically.

THE END

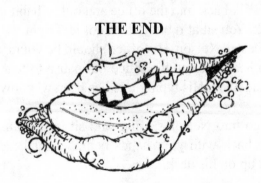

You fly back into the office, past glowing green typing drones that do not even look up. Nelson is still flexing his muscles and his jaw drops once he sees you. You plow into him, grabbing hold as the two of you smash through the office's wall into the hallway.

You roll on the ground holding Nelson close, hitting him again and again in the face. The blows leave large angry welts. His teeth fly through the air as you pummel him. You reach forward with both hands and grab the sides of his head. Your fingers break through bone and cartilage and you rip his head apart. You raise the hunks of dripping flesh, bone, and brain in the air, roaring with victory.

You realize that you are not yelling alone. All the other employees have come out and are cheering for you. Finally the cruel oppressor has been overtaken.

They all get to their knees and bow to you and your strength.

You stand up and stagger back from the corpse, dropping the hunks of what used to be Nelson's head. The employees are still on their knees, looking to you for guidance and direction.

Your gaze meets their eager eyes and you are not sure what to say.

You point back at their desks, "Get back to work. Those TPS Reports are not going to file themselves."

They scurry back to their workstations and you smile, pleased by their prompt response.

You walk back into the office and out of habit go over to your desk. You sit at it but it does not feel right.

You bested Nelson. His office should be yours, a spoil of war. You head back to his office but pause to tear the head off of Sanderson. His typing rate has been way lower than it should be.

You go into Nelson's office and sit in his plushy chair. You lean back with your hands behind your head and put your feet up on his desk.

You know what? You think you can get used to this.

You lean forward and page Ms. Matheson to bring you a cup of coffee.

THE END

Your workplace-approved haircut grows out to long smelly dreadlocks and your clothes morph into a patched-up mess of black and brown fabrics. You stand up straighter and prouder. There is so much wrong with the world and you have all the answers – if only those corporate pigs could put away their greed and listen to you.

You walk down the street and soon run into other people. You try to organize a march against our capitalist, racist, hetero-normative oppressors. You explain to them the emergency of our current situation, quoting Marx and Kropotkin, but the uneducated troglodytes do not understand the importance of what you are saying.

You flip them off and continue on your way.

Maybe the rest of the world will rise to your intellectual level at some point, until then you have your commune and benefit shows for causes that accomplish nothing.

One day the world will realize you were right all along. Until then, fuck 'em.

THE END

You round a corner and see that the noise came from a comic book store that has just burst into flames. The building, filled with paper and cardboard products of all sorts, is a raging inferno with flames pouring out from the front door and windows.

Two people stagger out of the building, their bodies completely engulfed.

Another person emerges from the building but appears to be completely unharmed. Even his clothes appear to be untouched by the scorching heat. He appears to be wearing a Star Trek uniform. You were never a fan of the show, too cheesy for your taste, but you recognize the costume. He's even wearing pointy ears to match the blue pajamas.

He lifts his hands above his head and points a hand at each of the burning people. Thick pillars of flames burst forth from his hands. The two people fall to the ground, finally dead.

He turns his head and sees you. Hate flares up in his eyes.

Uh oh.

Try talking to him, turn to page 142.
Go on the offensive. Attack! Turn to page 26.

You charge Mr. McWhiskers. Too much pain and loss has already been caused today. Humanity doesn't need your anti-government cat adding to the death toll.

You pick him up, "No! Bad cat!"

He hangs his head and purrs softly.

You can't stay mad at your kitty. You cuddle him against your chest and walk across the room, "It's OK, Mr. McWhiskers. I just can't have you overthrowing governments right now."

He purrs and, in one quick smooth motion, extends his claws and slits you right across the belly. Instantly your intestines unravel onto the floor. You fall to your knees, feeling so much lighter inside.

Mr. McWhiskers hops out of your arms and sits on the floor, his back to you. You see that a thick cord of intestine has gotten hooked by one of his jacket's chains. You try to speak and reach out but you no longer control your body.

Mr. McWhiskers scurries over to the control panel, dragging your insides across the floor. You watch in horror as you unravel across the bridge. The cord goes taut as the cat reaches the other side of the room and pulls the rest of your insides across the floor.

Fucking cat.

THE END

You don't want to leave your chances to wherever time and space may drop you off. You like having control of your destiny. You decide that it is your time to die but at least you will give the rest of the world a chance.

"A noble decision," says Farnsworth.

He turns back to the keyboard and starts typing.

After a minute he turns back to you, "The device will go off in ten seconds. You have any last words?"

You think hard. It has to be something good. Though it will not be recorded, you want to die knowing you went out with your head held high. Then it hits you, the perfect thing to say. The phrase that would truly cement this event and send you out on a high note.

"I –"

Too late.

THE END

You pick the door with the gun on it. That seems like the obvious best choice. You open the door and step into a room lined with racks of guns and explosives that go from the floor to the ceiling. There are handguns, machine guns, rifles, grenades, C-4, and a shit ton of other things that can blow things up.

You walk to the far wall in a daze, thrilled at your score. You grab a giant gun off the rack that is almost as big as you. You can barely hold the massive weapon.

The door slams open behind you.

You spin around and there are two people standing in the doorway, each clad all in black. They have huge Mohawks. One has a handgun. The other is holding out human intestines wrapped around his hands like piano wire.

You don't even think. You pull the trigger, sending a barrage of bullets at the punks. In a split second, you lose control of the gun as its kickback knocks you to the ground. Bullets spray and bounce around the room. In the entirety of Complex 23 this is probably the worst place for you to lose control of a high-powered machine gun.

One bullet nicks a package of C-4 and half of the Complex is engulfed in an explosion. Fortunately, it happens so fast that you feel no pain as your body is blown into thousands of tiny bits.

THE END

The coin comes up heads so you go left. You slosh over to the door. Mr. McWhiskers flies behind you. Hovering a foot above the floor, careful not to get his paws wet.

The door has a big red button next to it on the wall. You push the button and the door slides open, just like something out of *Star Trek*. Maybe that poster does make sense.

You step through and find yourself in a large room of computer banks and about a dozen aliens. They are all wearing identical silver jumpsuits with their heads and hands exposed. Their skin is cracked and bright red – like that of burn victims.

The entire far wall is a giant view screen. Right now it is displaying a building toppling over from the saucer's ray blasts. You see burning people falling like leaves from its windows.

This must be the bridge of the ship. Facing the screen one of the aliens sits in a large chair. It is the captain's chair. The captain stands up and points at you. His speech sounds like gargling wasps.

The aliens charge you.

Mr. McWhiskers flies out from behind you and immediately decapitates the nearest alien with his super-sized claws.

You rush an alien and punch him in the stomach. Your fist shoots straight through, splattering thick milky goo all over you. As you pull your fist back, you grab hold of the thing's spine and pull it out.

The alien falls over and you spin around, swinging the bone. You hit another invader, shattering its spine and head. In moments, you and Mr. McWhiskers have utterly destroyed all the aliens except for the captain.

The captain stands firm. He is not backing down from you.

Attack the captain, turn to page 32.
Try to negotiate peace with the captain, turn to page 164.

This is the moment you've been waiting for. You've dreamed of this moment for years. You are finally leading the vicious attack on your uncaring oppressor.

"Fellow anthropoids –"

You stop when you see that no one is looking at you. They are all looking in the same direction, toward the side of the office. You spin around and look at Supervisor Nelson – he is paying you no mind and is staring away as well.

You turn to see what deprived you of your moment of glorious victory. Everyone is staring out the windows and you see that the sky outside has turned a deep shade of purple.

You turn back to your acolytes, "People! Focus!"

They all snap to attention.

"Focus your energy, your rage, on Nelson! He is who deserves it!"

They cheer and charge Nelson.

Nelson roars at the charging horde like a caged animal. His muscles bulge out, tearing his clothes in a dozen places. He looks just like a white collar Incredible Hulk.

He glares at all of you with glowing red eyes. He snorts, shooting black smoke out of his nose.

"I'm going to give you all one chance," he bellows, "get back to work!"

You turn back to your followers to rally them for an attack but there is nothing behind you but the water cooler. You turn completely around, confused.

You see that they are now all back at their desks, their weapons abandoned, typing on their computers at an inhuman speed, their hands little more than blurs. There is a strange green glow coming off of them.

You are not backing down so easily. You assume a fighting stance and let out a war yell that would make Rambo proud.

Supervisor Nelson flexes at you.

You charge. You are half way across the room when the entire building shakes and you are thrown to the floor. You look over and see a massive eye peaking in through the window. The monster is here!

One problem at a time.

You race toward Nelson, ready to pound his head in, when two giant claws the size of compact cars burst through the walls. The claws sway about for a moment and then quickly snap forward.

You dive as one just misses your head.

The other workers keep typing.

The claw furthest from you catches a worker – you think his name is Stephen but you could be wrong. It begins to drag him away from his computer but he holds onto his desk with surprising strength and keeps updating the database.

Finally the claw tears him from his workstation. He begins to thrash and scream, trying to pull himself free.

You stare in horror as the claw pulls Stephen – yeah, you're sure it's Stephen – toward the thing's terrible mouth.

The monster's head reminds you of a massive centipede. Its mouth has two large claws protruding from the side, flexing and eager for food. Thick green slime drips down its chin.

Stephen screams and struggles as the monster brings him to its mouth. The claws on the side dart forward and pull in the man. The screaming abruptly stops and is replaced with crunching bones and clicking keyboards.

The monster swallows with a loud gulp and the claws come tearing back into the office.

Attack the monster, turn to page 43.
Attack Supervisor Nelson, turn to page 108.

You back away from Solok, ready to attack if you have to.

The spaceman's ray gun has transformed Solok. He now has large gauged earlobes to go with the rubber points. There is one hoop through his lower left lip and two hoops through his right eyebrow. His previously tight, well-kept hair is now a jet-black, spiky mess.

His clothing has even changed. The Star Trek insignia on his uniform, that weird triangle thingy with a circle around it, has moved so it is now an A with a circle around it. Anarchy. Around the ends of his shirt sleeves and pants legs run rows of metal spikes.

He wipes his face with his hands. You see that his fingernails are now painted black.

"Whoah, what the fuck happened to me?"

He looks up and sees your defensive position.

"It's OK. I'm not going to attack you," he says.

You relax. His mind has not been turned into a murderer.

You walk over to him, "Damn, that really did a number on you." You look him up and down. "I think it's an improvement."

He sarcastically smiles at you and then looks confused. "Do you hear that?"

"Hear wh–" you stop when you feel the duel rhythmic thumps. Oh shit, you know what this means.

As if on cue, hordes of people spill out onto your street, fleeing and flying past. Many of them have been changed into some punk version of their former selves.

Quickly, the pounding becomes very loud. A few blocks down, a row of buildings crash to the ground. In the midst of the destruction, there is a great roar.

The smoke clears, revealing the biggest thing you have ever seen. In many ways it looks like a kind of giant crocodile. It's on all fours and covered with green scales that glisten in the daylight. Instead of lizard-like legs, the thing's legs are thick with knotty muscle. The front pair bends out like a bulldog. Its face is flat like a primate's except for its massive snout that juts forward. Its head is taller than any building around and the body is at least two blocks long.

It looks at a crowd of people fleeing before it and drools. It slams its face into the ground, scooping up concrete, wrecked cars, and people into its mouth. It lazily chews as flesh, stone, and metal fall to the ground beneath it.

People are running past you trying to get away from the creature.

You grab Solok's arm, "I think we need to get out of here."

He doesn't answer and looks to the beast which is now starting to slowly lumber in your direction.

"I have a plan," he finally says.

See what Solok's plan is, turn to page 104.
Fuck that, we gotta get outta here!!! Turn to page 111.

You decide to follow Farnsworth. With everything that is going down around here it would be best to not be alone. Besides, he's a living scientific genesis. It will be a hell of a story to tell later.

You follow him into the passageway and the door slides shut behind you. Farnsworth waddles ahead of you, leading the way.

"Where are we going," you ask.

"I have a backup lab hidden in the building," he responds, "just for times like this."

He leads you down several winding hallways. You've worked in Complex 23 for years and had no knowledge of these passageways.

It does not take long for you to come to another door. Farnsworth opens it and motions you through.

You find yourself in a massive room. Three walls are lined with elaborate computer systems, monitors, and keyboards. The other wall is nothing but television screens displaying images from all over the complex. On one of them a giant spider sucking a man dry. You quickly look away.

Farnsworth walks over to one of the keyboards and starts typing.

"Things are bad, real bad," he says, "the entire complex has been compromised. To the best of my knowledge, this is the only secure location left. Our entire defensive system has been deactivated and evacuation attempts have proven unsuccessful.

"The attackers in question appear to be an invading force from another planet. Not only are they attacking this complex, but my monitoring of world media outlets has confirmed they have launched a full scale attack on the entire planet.

"To make matters worse, they are stealing the experiments from this island and letting them loose throughout the Earth. They are also using some kind of technology to make our experiments even larger and more aggressive. I can't explain it but it seems to be based on the same principle that gives their rayguns the ability to transform humans.

"Fortunately, I have anticipated some kind of disaster like this and have been developing some responses. Only two are operational at this time."

He turns around and takes off his glasses. He absent-mindedly cleans them with his shirt and says, "I'm afraid neither work out that well for us."

"The first option is what I call the 'Super-Maker.' By releasing several thousand tons of gene-rewriting gas into the air, every normal human on Earth will gain super-powers. What the powers are exactly will vary from person to person, but it should give the human race a fighting chance.

"When the gases are released into the atmosphere they will turn the sky a lovely shade of purple the whole world over. The problem is that we will not be here to see that. The propulsion unit uses so much energy that it will overload Complex 23's power station and destroy everything on the island, including us.

"The second option is a device that I recently acquired from a Dr. Taylor in London. It is a device that transports its users through time and space. We can travel back to before this disaster. The problem is that we will retain no memory of what has happened and we are not guaranteed to even be ourselves at the other end. We could end up as anyone from anytime. I was hoping to work out the kinks of the machine before it was ever used but I don't think I'll get my chance to do that.

"I'm so happy you showed up. You can decide which plan I should go with. I've been putting off making a decision as I'm just a scientist. I invent and study these things. It's not my job to take responsibility for their use. So, what should we do?"

Do you want to sacrifice yourself to give what is left of humanity a fighting chance? Turn to page 85.
Do you want to take your chances traveling back through time and space, turn to page 169.

You are awoken some time later as you are tossed out of bed and sirens fill your head. You try to get to your feet but are knocked down again as the ship rocks violently. You brace yourself against the walls and make it out of your room and up to the deck to see what is happening.

Towering out of the water, hundreds of feet into the sky, is a demon. It has a very human body from the waist up. Large twisted horns protrude from its forehead and its body is covered with red scales. Its arms are raised and it flexes huge muscles at the ship.

The battleship fires its guns at the thing. As the shells bounce off the thick hide, it laughs deep and long. It winds back a giant fist and punches the side of the ship. As you hear the sound of metal bending and breaking, your heart drops.

Someone grabs you from behind and pulls you toward the back of the ship. You want to turn and see who and why but you cannot look away from this hellish vision. This is not one of the creations from the island, this is some kind of brand new horror. You are thrown onto a lifeboat that has three other sailors on it.

"Hold on," says one of them as he pulls a rope the boat drops twenty feet straight down into the water.

You manage not to fall out. You watch from the lifeboat as the demon pummels on the battleship until it is smashed to pieces and sinks beneath the water. The demon then disappears underwater after the ship.

The four of you seem to be in the only lifeboat to escape. You all look and yell for other survivors to no avail. It is then you all realize that there are no supplies and no oars for the boat. You sit wordlessly and wait for help that you know will not come.

Turn to page 51.

You fly off in the direction of your office. You have always wanted the chance to put Supervisor Nelson in his place and now, with Mr. McWhiskers as your backup, you know you can.

Quickly you are back at your former corporate prison. You and Mr. McWhiskers hover outside the windows, peeking in. All the workers are still hunched over their keyboards, typing at an inhuman speed. The green glow from them is brighter than when you left. You don't see Nelson anywhere. The door to his office is closed. He must be behind it.

You slowly open a window, careful to make as little noise as possible, and climb through. Mr. McWhiskers follows you inside and quickly scuttles under a nearby desk. None of the workers notice. They are too super-absorbed in their work.

Surprise is your biggest advantage. Nelson is not going to see this attack coming.

Then Nelson bursts out of his office and yells, "Why is my supervisor-sense tingling?" His eyes dart about the room and then lock on you. He roars like a bull that has been hit in the balls, and charges you with as much strength.

You brace for the attack and he slams you straight to the ground. He pounds your face with his fists and the room starts to go black.

You hear a mew of fury and Mr. McWhiskers bursts out from under a nearby desk – kitty surprise attack! He flies between Nelson and you. With one paw of razor-sharp claws he neatly disembowels Nelson. He hooks a hunk of intestine with the claws on the other paw.

Mr. McWhiskers flies around Nelson several times, each go-around pulling out more of your former boss' guts. Nelson begins to lose strength as Mr. McWhiskers wraps the intestines around that asshole's neck.

Blood dripping in your eyes, you lean up, grab the intestines and pull tight. Nelson's face goes blue and he drops to the ground. Mr. McWhiskers dives for the gaping wound in his stomach and has a snack.

Supervisor Nelson manages to croak out, "You're fired." His neck makes a terrible crack and he gurgles.

You pull yourself to your feet while Mr. McWhiskers continues gorging himself.

You look around the room and suddenly find all the other employees on their knees, bowing down before you. You have conquered the cruel oppressor. You are their new leader.

Benevolently release your fellow office drones to pursue their own goals in life, turn to page 48.

Assume your rightful place as ruler of these mindless drones, turn to page 68.

You sigh and pick up the next TPS Report. You need to get through these. The company doesn't pay you twenty-five cents over minimum wage for nothing.

You load up the database on your computer and start transferring the information. Everything is going fine until you come across a number that you can't make out. It is either a six or a five but you cannot tell from the handwriting. You check the name on the bottom to see who filled out the form. It was Margaret. She has terrible handwriting and you can never be sure what she is trying to communicate.

Unfortunately, Margaret is out sick today. You can't ask her what it says. You don't like leaving a form uncompleted so you decide to guess.

Assume that it is a six, turn to page 20.
Assume that it is a five, turn to page 161.

Ten years later…

You stand on top a hill of sand and rubble. You look to the dirty purple sky and see the angry green clouds. Rain is coming. Thank God. You can't remember the last time you had a drink.

Your cloak of tanned human hide whips against your body. A part of you still shivers at the feel of it. But there is no shortage of corpses and you need clothes.

You take out your Walkman, a prize from the last raid, and put the headphones on your head. You push play and CIV fills your ears.

In the distance is a city. You don't know what it was once called. You don't care, it doesn't matter anymore. You can see saucers hovering over it and large shapes moving within the blackened and burned skeleton buildings.

You turn back and look at your army. Over ten-thousand strong, you have been going from town to town and city to city gathering those who survived and have been changed. You are hoping one day to have a large enough force to take back the planet.

A cat flies up from the mass of people and circles your head, its long gray hair pulled tight against its body. The strange animal seems to be the only nonhuman to have been changed and has been your best friend for the past five years.

You turn back to the city and listen to the song, focusing on the lyrics, pumping yourself up for another attack.

"Can't wait one more minute!"

The cat – his tag says "Mr. McWhiskers," but you could never bring yourself to call him that – flexes ten-inch-long claws as it looks to the city. You can see bloodlust in his eyes.

Today will be another long day of death and violence. Just like yesterday was and tomorrow will be.

But that's the world you know and live in.

You turn up the music and smile, already salivating at the thought of fighting and killing.

Better make the best of it.

THE END

This is the moment you've been waiting for. You've always known the shit was going to hit the fan at some point. You admit that you weren't expecting intergalactic border-jumpers, but if that's the hand God is going to deal, than that's how you'll play.

You are the only human being for a hundred miles around, your fortress buried deep in the wilderness. The first two saucers that flew overhead surely weren't expecting there to be any human resistance way out here. The surface-to-air missiles took them out quickly.

You monitor the global situation from your underground bunker. One by one, all of your global contacts disappeared as well as all the media outlets. Any saucer that comes nearby is shot down by your defensive system. The few giant creatures that come by are quickly cut to shreds by your patrolling gang of ninja robots.

It soon becomes clear that you are the only person left. If anyone is going to take care of these alien bastards, it will have to be you.

You consider what your best course of action should be.

Use the super secret weapon, turn to page 147.
Use the secret super weapon, turn to page 66.

Nelson is crazy. That is plain to you now. He's the captain of this sinking corporate ship and he's going down with the boat.

But not with you.

You spend a few moments drafting a manifesto and then print it out on the company letterhead. You want it to be legally valid of course. You collect them from the printer and walk desk to desk passing them out.

It reads:

```
To my co-oarsmen on this corporate barge:

        It has come to my attention that
our current leader and captain wishes
to drive us upon the rocky shores.
He does not operate out of malice or
deceit but out of a misguided sense
of duty to our regional overlords.
I propose a modest solution, that
we take up arms and overthrow this
Ahab of the commercial armada. At
precisely 11:14 I will drop my pen
to the floor and make an elaborate
show of it. This is a signal to all
of you to gather in the break room
where we will then devise a strategy
of resistance.

Yours in struggle,
John Smithe
```

You sit back at your desk after everyone has received the notice. You look at the clock, 11:13. You stare intently at it until it changes to 11:14.

You stand from your desk, get on top of your chair and leap up into the air. You flip backwards and do a spilt in midair, all those years of gymnastics lessons your parents forced you to take are finally paying off. You stick the landing and hold your arms out.

Everyone in the office is staring at you.

Oh shit, you forgot about the pen. You hastily reach forward and brush your pen off your desk. You somehow manage to knock yourself off balance in the process and you tumble to the floor with the pen.

As you get to your feet you see everyone in the office getting up from their desks and moving to the break room. You look back at Nelson's office but his door is still shut with no sign of awareness of the current uprising.

You rush to the break room with a sense of power you have never felt in your life. You are now shepherd of these sheeple.

Turn to page 29.

"So what's your plan?"

Solok doesn't answer at first. "Don't grieve for me, this is logical."

You eye him suspiciously, "Solok, what are you going to do?"

He stares without emotion at the monster. He finally says, "The needs of the many..."

"...Outweigh the needs of the few," you finish.

"Or the one," he says, still looking at the monster. Solok turns to you, "I always have been and always will be your friend."

He brings up his right hand, curled in a fist, and raises his index and pinky fingers – flashing you devil horns. "Live long and prosper."

"What…"

Solok turns from you and jogs towards the beast.

"Solok, what are you doing?" He does not respond.

He runs straight at the monstrosity.

The thing was still lumbering forward at a slow but extremely destructive pace, each movement toppling over buildings. Its gargantuan paws flattening cars and people with each step. The few who are attempting to engage the beast in battle with their powers are not even slowing it. The behemoth roars and even though you are three blocks away, you can smell the thick stink of fish.

Solok is now right in front of it. He stops and looks fearlessly up at the monster. Suddenly there is a huge burst of flames at his feet and he flies though the air straight into the thing's mouth and then he is gone, swallowed whole.

"What the fuck," you yell to no one, "that was your great plan?"

The thing stops moving and goes very still. Its head starts slowly swaying back and forth and a low groan comes from it. The bass is so deep you can feel your bones shaking.

The monster's midsection starts to swell out, like someone is inflating a giant balloon inside the beast. You can hear the skin stretching and internal bones snapping as the midsection grows to larger and larger proportions. It is almost comical when none of the thing's four legs are even touching the ground anymore.

Then there is a *POP* so loud that the noise itself knocks you over. A gigantic ball of fire rise up into the air from where the monster used to be. The monster is now nothing more than a billion tiny bits, flying through the air in every direction. Parts of it will probably end up miles away.

Then the blood hits you. You are completely drenched with thick black tar that smells oddly of watermelon.

You stand, disgusted, and shake the gunk off your hands and wipe the shit off your face. Pieces of the monster are falling all around you but none of them are bigger than your fist.

PLOP. PLOP. PLOP, is the sound of the wet hunks of flesh falling around you.

There's a loud *THUNK* at your feet you look down. It's Solok's head. He is even still wearing the pointy ears. On his face is a frozen a snarl of defiance.

You fall to your knees and pick up his head. You hold it up high in the air with one hand while the other flashes the devil horns.

"Sssssssoooollllllloooooookkk," you scream to the heavens.

You go silent and toss the head back to the ground.

You look at the street around you. It is covered with gore and hunks of monster flesh. Almost no building is left completely intact and dozens of fires are burning freely. There are small groups of people milling about the streets. Some are even flying through the air. Judging from the powers on display and the fact so many people are still alive, you assume they have all been changed as well.

Welcome to the rest of your life.

Turn to page 98.

You decide to take on the flying saucers. They are the ones responsible for all this meaningless death and destruction and you've had enough. You're going to bring the fight to them.

You and Mr. McWhiskers fly over the city looking for your target. Beneath you everything is burning and you can see roving gangs moving through the streets. It is pure chaos.

You quickly come upon one of the saucers hovering in the air and shooting its death rays at the people and buildings below. You slam into the hull and break through.

Mr. McWhiskers follows.

You find yourself in a dark hallway. Most of the light is coming through the hole you created. The walls are made of some weird pink and spongy material that looks organic, like a skinned dog. There is half a foot of some unknown clear liquid covering the floor.

On the wall in front of you there is a poster for the J.J. Abrams *Star Trek* movie, crudely taped up. You approach the poster slowly. You are very confused. Why would aliens be *Star Trek* fans?

Never mind that now.

You look to your left and right. There are doors on either side of you.

You take a coin out of your pocket. You can't think of a better way to decide where to go. Heads, left. Tails, right.

Find a coin and flip it.

Turn to page 87.

Turn to page 64.

You set your sights back on Nelson and charge. He braces and when you collide, he grabs you, lifts you off the ground, spins around three times, and throws you at the window the attacking creature is looking through.

You fly through the air and smash through the glass. You keep traveling and go right through the monster's eye. You can feel the cornea give in and then break. You become quickly soaked with eye goo.

You body keeps going through the thing's brain and you burst out the back of the skull, sending bone fragments, gray

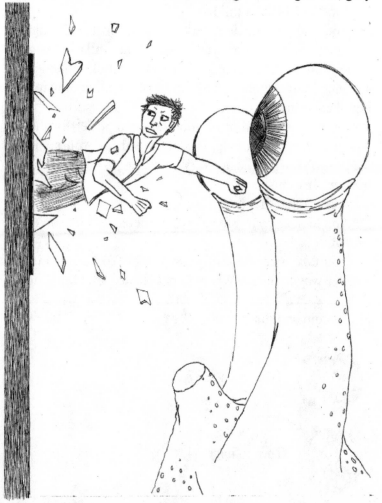

matter, and blood spraying into the air.

You close your eyes and prepare for the long fall to the ground but it never happens, you don't have any sensation of falling. You open your eyes and find yourself hovering in the air, covered in dripping pink and grey pulp.

The thing has a huge hole in the back of its head. Through the hole you can see Nelson flipping you off. The beast wavers for a moment and then crumbles to the ground, its massive girth toppling the buildings it falls onto.

You hover in the air amazed at your new ability to fly. You look over and inspect your body. It appears to be unharmed, albeit covered in viscera and stinking like sewage.

You look up into the sky and admire its new purple tone. Despite everything that has happened today, you feel good. You feel full of power. This is a new day.

Fly back to the office to continue fighting Supervisor Nelson, turn to page 80.

Fly off to start a new life with these new powers, turn to page 33.

You stand on the bridge of the Galganex, the mothership of the invasion fleet. Before you is a wall of view screens. Each screen displaying a new devastation every twenty seconds. Your eyes dart around and you laugh to yourself. It was so easy to turn the planet, and even humans themselves, against humanity. All it took was a little genetic rewiring and there was instant planet-wide panic, destruction, and death.

This is a truly glorious day for the empire. You will have many decorations awaiting you when you return home.

Human life is already extinct on three of the planet's continents. You better get down there soon if you want to get in on the fun.

You take the turbolift to the hangar bay. There, you put on a spacesuit to protect yourself from the Earth's dangerous atmospheric pressure. You board one of the saucers and fly down to the Earth.

Your ship flies high in the atmosphere but even from up here you can see the glow of the fires on the ground, their black pillars of smoke rising around you.

You ask the navigator to locate a high concentration of human survivors and are quickly given coordinates. In moments, the saucer is hovering above the surviving infestation.

Fly around in your ship and rain death from above, turn to page 57.
Land and get your hands dirty, turn to page 162.

"Man you're crazy, we gotta go!"

You pull on his shoulder to indicate that he should start running. He looks at the monster once more and then to you. He nods and you both join the crowds fleeing down the street away from the monster.

The beast follows. You look over your shoulder and see that the monster is quickly gaining on you. It may not be moving fast but it is just so big that it catches up with ease.

The monster's next step is so close it shakes the ground beneath you. When it steps forward again, everyone, including you and Solok, get thrown about two feet and come crashing to the ground.

You land on your back and see the beast's head plunging forward, straight at you. You scramble to your feet and dash to the side of the road. Its jaws tear the road and claim another dozen victims.

You spin your head around. Where's Solok?

You look up to the beast and see Solok's corpse sticking half out of the monster's mouth.

The thing chews a few times, you have to dodge falling debris, and then it starts to move forward again, ignoring you.

The redwood-sized back legs stomp down on the street. Far too close for your liking. Nearby cars and rubble bounce from the aftershock. You hide behind a mass of broken concrete, hoping to avoid becoming a smear on the thing's foot.

What you don't see is the thing's tail crash into you when your back is turned. The tail is bigger and thicker than a train and it carries you straight into a nearby building. The building crumbles from the force of the tail, spilling tons of building material straight down on top of you.

Turn to page 62.

You realize that you cannot stay here. That monster is getting too close and if Supervisor Nelson has his way you'll be trapped here until that beast violates the building and knocks it over.

You crouch down in the cubical and crawl out. You race from cubical to cubical keeping your eyes on Nelson's office door. Your coworkers pay you no mind as you rush from workspace to workspace. They are too involved with their individual projects.

You make it to the exit and go through.

You rush over to elevator and take it to the lobby. You run outside and the fresh air hits you.

Once out you are not sure what to do. Your apartment is on the other side of the city and you seriously doubt that the bus lines are running. You need to go there before you try escaping from the city, the giant monsters, attacking flying saucers. Someone has to rescue, Mr. McWhiskers, your wonderful gray long hair cat.

You see no choice but to walk. Hopefully you will be able to avoid painful death.

You head down the streets for home, the sound of gun shots and the smell of fire in the air.

You round a corner and pause when you see, in the center of the road, a person dressed in a full body white spacesuit and a helmet with a dark black visor. The spaceman is walking down the street holding what looks to be a cheesy raygun from an old Sci-Fi movie. The gun shoots black beams. One of those beams hits a middle age woman dressed in a blue flower-print dress and she changes into a spiky hair freak. Her clothing mutates to black leather and she runs off shouting.

The spaceman turns and aims his gun at you. You freeze, terrified, and have no chance to avoid the beam.

When it hits you can feel the very fabric of your reality being rewritten. No longer do you crave the soothing saxophone of Kenny G, you crave music with anger, something with screaming. You feel your clothes change and hair transform.

The beam is rewriting your DNA. You become punker than your parents ever feared.

Put down this book and go dig out an old board game. Grab a six-sided die from it and then come back.

Roll the die to see what type of punk you turn into.

A dirty, drunken street punk, turn to page 25.

A muscle-bound skinhead, turn to page 140.

A political anarcho punk, turn to page 82.

A vegan and edge kid, turn to page 114.

A sensitive emo kid, turn to page 50.

???? Turn to page 127.

Your hair is reduced to a tight buzz cut. Your work clothes mutate to camo-shorts and an Earth Crisis T-shirt.

You are no longer concerned with your own safety but are overcome with sadness at the cruel torture animals undergo beneath their human oppressors.

Your muscles bulge beneath your clothes. Because you've never drank or gotten high you have become addicted to working out.

You walk down the street while you sing Minor Threat songs to yourself under your breath. You soon come upon a restaurant that fills you with rage. The people that frequent this place are soldiers against you in the war of animal liberation.

You pick up a trashcan and hurl it through the windows, shattering the glass.

You climb through the hole and pull out your lighter. You may not smoke but you always have a light on you for this purpose. You set fire to the table inside. Let's see how these peddlers of death like a taste of their own medicine.

While you are wrapped up in this act of destruction the poor immigrant owner sneaks up behind you with a meat cleaver. He tearfully drives the blade into the back of your skull. He does not want to hurt you but you have given him no other choice. You have threatened his livelihood.

You were so concerned with the little animals that you never stopped to think about the other implications your actions may have. So now you are laying on the ground bleeding to death from a massive head wound.

Serves you right, you selfish bastard.

THE END

You turn from the punk massacre and let out a war cry that would make even Henry Rollins proud.

You brandish fresh spikes and charge the massive thing.

It sees you coming and thrashes tentacles into buildings, sending glass and concrete flying through the air and down upon its attackers. A guy with a shaved head, massive gauged ears, and a torn Fucked Up shirt runs next to you. A chunk of building the size of a small car lands right on him, grinding him into the street and splattering you with gore.

You get to it and start stabbing at the massive pink tentacles. Your spikes sink easily into the beast's flesh. Thick and creamy green ooze leaks from the wounds and the creature roars. The air stinks of eggs and infection.

Another tentacle shoots out from behind you and snatches you up. You try stabbing at it but you are stuffed into the creature's mouth too quickly – you don't even have a chance to react.

It takes a lot of chewing for you to die.

THE END

You go to the break room and pour coffee into one of the common-use coffee cups. Above the coffee pot is an inspirational poster. It is a picture of a hang glider with a sunset background. It reads, "Passion: Live daringly, boldly, fearlessly."

You remember a point in your life when you had passion but that's not for you anymore. Dreams and desires are for the naivety of youth. The real world is something else. You've learned to recognize that over the years.

Turn to page 97.

You push through the door with the angry beast face on it. You're not sure what the logo means but you hope this is a lab devoted to special monster killing weapons.

The room is lined with counters and computers and papers are scattered about. On the walls are posters and printouts related to the monsters and their environments. In the center of the room is a large metal chair with wires leading from it to a computer bank in the back of the room. Above the chair, hanging from the ceiling by a mass of thick cables, is what looks like a Sci-Fi version of a motorcycle helmet.

You walk around the room picking up papers and glancing at diagrams on walls. It looks very similar to your workstation. This appears to be a room dedicated to studying the habits of the monsters. You even see some reports you've written.

You go to the back of the room and to the computer station the chair is hooked up to. A quick scan of the notes reveals that scientists in this lab were working on a device that transfers the consciousness of a human into one of the experiments. A giant monster consciously controlled by a human – this is the weapon you've been looking for.

You boot up the computer and quickly load the programs associated with the consciousness transfer. It's pretty easy for you to navigate– you're surprised to find out how much of the work you have done yourself.

The machine locates three creatures to which you may transfer your consciousness. The system identifies the beasts in strange code that is a mystery to you - one beast is labeled "BN5G6." You summon your courage. Extreme times call for extreme measures.

You set the computer to one of the random creatures and go over to the chair. You sit in the uncomfortable cold steel and pull down the helmet. It has a chin-strap that secures tightly in place.

Behind you, the computer system kicks to life as the transfer process begins. You expect pain or some unpleasant feeling but instead your vision turns bright purple. Your skin feels like it is being licked by a hundred cats and then you are whisked away.

Go grab a pack of playing cards and shuffle the deck. Flip over the top card. If it is a

Spade, turn to page 121.

Club, turn to page 60.

Heart, turn to page 168.

Diamond, draw another card.

You may be a cruel God but you do reward those who live to serve you. If it were not for those that have kept your memory alive, you would have faded to the dreamland of dead Gods long ago.

Besides, their treachery against their own species amuses you.

You come out of the water and tower over your worshipers, a behemoth come to land. The insects cower before you.

You roar and their minds shatter. They run off drooling and jabbering into the vermin nest. They will spread the news of your glorious return.

You knock over several of the structures around you and form a crude throne out of the ruins. You sit upon it and the sky turns a dark scarlet.

You twitch your tentacles and the seas begins the boil
This world is yours.

THE END

You open your eyes and find yourself standing in the center of a city looking down at the tops of buildings. You examine your body and find you're covered in green scales. You have two massive legs and two stubby arms. You feel large spines running down your back and your tail waving with your girth. Your tail crashes into a building and you shake your whole body.

An animal scream causes you to spin around. You see a huge gorilla, just as large as you, charging. It runs on all fours, its feet and hands tossing people and cars aside and smashing into surrounding buildings.

It stops about two blocks from you and stands up straight. The beast throws back its head and unleashes a primal war cry. It beats its chest, adding a drum rhythm.

You open your mouth. A bright blue beam shoots out and hits the ape in the face. The monster's head explodes, spraying blood, bone, and brains into the air. The corpse sways for a moment and then collapses to the ground, taking down two buildings with it.

You roar victoriously.

You notice a loud thumping sound coming closer. You turn and look around and see a small fleet of helicopters approaching. You try speaking to them, to tell them that you are on their side, but only beastly growls come out.

The helicopters are getting closer and they look ready for a fight.

Try finding another way to signal them, turn to page 151.
It's you or them. Kill them, turn to page 42.

Everyone laughed at you when you started building the ship. No one believed that you received the directions from the spirit of William Shatner. You know he's not dead but that made the apparition even weirder and more worthy of your attention. He gave you very detailed directions very slowly and warned you of an impending disaster that would threaten all of humanity.

They all called you crazy but you continued working, determined to fulfill your divine duty.

You completed the ship just one week ago.

When the aliens showed up you knew it had something to do with your mission, but the project did not make complete sense. When the giant monsters showed up, it all fell into place.

You rushed into the backyard where the ship was kept. You jumped into the cockpit and fired up the engines.

The ship rose several feet into the air, stretching and flexing its fingers. Building a flying ship to resemble a giant hand seemed really strange, but who are you to question Shatner? You followed the directions exactly, except for the fingernails. You made them purple because you think purple is pretty.

You set the coordinates for the city and fly off.

The city is a mess of rubble and flames. You never cared much for it, too much noise and too many people. The cause of all this devastation lumbers ahead of you.

The thing looks like a dragon walking upright. Instead of the classic monster head from western and eastern myth, the beast has a squid at the end of its neck.

Your ship circles the thing. It strikes at you with tentacles and claws but you are too fast and agile to be hit. You buzz around it, seeking the best spot to strike.

A hint of metal shines on the thing's back – there's your target. Discretely poking out from between the beast's scales, you see a zipper slider.

Your ship darts forward and the mechanical fingers

grab hold. The ship shoots down and unzips the seam. The creature's back opens like a jacket and a tidal wave of blood and monstrous organs rush out. The thing stops moving and its body collapses in on itself like a balloon animal being deflated.

Your ship hovers over the massive carcass. The thing is no longer moving. You are sure it's dead.

You set the ship's coordinates for the next city. There are many more beasts to battle and people to save. The world is counting on you.

THE END

The punk charges and something inside of you snaps. You see that poor girl dying in front of you. You see the mangled corpses.

You stand firm as the monster of a man charges you. He has both his arms raised ready to strike.

When he is almost on top of you, you dash forward and raise the staple gun to your attacker's face. There is a brief moment when surprise flashes across his face but then you pull the trigger two times, firmly planting an industrial grade staple into each of his eyes.

He drops both his weapons and falls to his knees. He raises his hands to his face but they do not get near his wounds. His eyelids did not have time to close before you pulled the trigger and the staples are jutting crudely out from a mess of white, creamy goo now running down his cheeks.

The man starts to scream like a dying rabbit and your whole world goes red. You pick up the bone saw from the floor and start screaming as well. Your yells are not of pain or fear but of rage.

You grab him by the hair and pull his head back, exposing his neck. With your other hand you grid the saw across his throat. Blood splatters across your face and the teeth of the saw get caught in his flesh. His screams hit a higher pitch and volume.

You work harder, sawing back and forth as blood sprays across face and body and your screaming overtakes his. At some point you realize he has gone silent and limp. You drop the body to the ground and stop screaming.

You pick the staple gun back up in one hand, still holding on to the bone saw with the other, and stand hunched over in the hallway trying to catch your breath and listen for others coming.

After what must have been five minutes or five hours you finally have control of yourself again. You hear no signs of anything else so you head for the exit door and go through it.

The sun and heat on the other side immediately surprises

you and makes the blood covering your body sticky. You smell gunpowder and smoke in the air and hear screams, inhuman roars, and the sounds of battle in the distance.

In front of you are one hundred yards of sand and then a thick wall of jungle that surrounds Complex 23 on three sides. On the forth side is a port and a river that leads out into open sea.

You look left and right but see only the walls of the massive complex stretching off for hundreds of yards and jungle. You take a moment to gather your sense of direction and then head off toward the docks.

Turn to page 18.

126

You slam against the door and it does not budge.

You throw yourself against it again, putting all your strength into it, and the door flies open. You fall through and tumble to the ground.

All the windows of the shop have been boarded up. The only light is coming from several movie-shoot-style lamps. In the center of the room is a large tarp. On the tarp is a woman who looks like she's spent many years on the street doing more than one type of blow. She's giving oral sex to a pig.

Looking at their faces, you can't tell which of them is enjoying this less.

There is a man on one side of the room with a digital video camera. He moves around the scene, capturing the grotesque display. Flanking him are two very large men in black suits. They hold pistols.

All three turn to you in shock. The woman stops, swine cock still in mouth, and stares. Even the pig stares.

The two armed men rush forward. One shuts and boards up the door. The other puts the barrel of his gun to your head.

"What the fuck you doin' in here?" he asks.

You try to talk but only weak whines come out.

The building shakes as the monster walks outside.

"Damn storm," says the man at the door.

They don't know what's going on.

You start to cry and try to talk but the man with the gun slams the butt of his weapon into your temple.

You fall and somewhere distant you hear pig squeals.

Turn to page 79.

There must have been something messed up with that spaceman's gun. When the beam hits you, you suddenly sprout a cowboy hat on your head. You clothes change to jeans and a brown vest.

The spaceman cocks his head at you, puzzled over your transformation.

He fires the gun again as you spit out some chewing tobacco.

Roll the die again and you become...

⚀ A dirty, drunken street punk, turn to page 25.

⚁ A muscle-bound skinhead, turn to page 140.

⚂ A political anarcho punk, turn to page 82.

⚃ A vegan and edge kid, turn to page 114.

⚄ A sensitive emo kid, turn to page 50.

⚅ Roll again.

You sit down at the computer and within minutes hack into the mainframe and have access to literally every computer system in the building. At your command, all the automatic locks seal on every door and main power and communication are restored.

There is so much to do. You need to find out how many people are still alive in the building, how to permanently stop the killers that are now locked in various rooms, how to regain control of the experiments, and how to stop the flying saucers from attacking. And that's just what has to be done right now.

You need to be able to work quicker.

An idea immediately pops to mind. You hate it but you see no other choice.

You scan the room and see a scalpel lying next to a rat cage. You rush over and grab it. There are various other medical instruments scattered about and you ruffle through them until you find one of those small rubber hammers doctors use to test reflexes. You take that too.

You dig through desks until you find a small compact mirror and you race back to the computer. You set up the mirror and, without giving yourself time to think about what you are doing, you take the scalpel to your forehead and cut deep. Blood and pain overwhelm your vision as you make four long incisions. A neatly cut square of flesh falls off your forehead, revealing the white skull beneath.

You put the scalpel against the bone like a stake and pick up the hammer. You strike the blunt end of the scalpel.

CRACK!

You fall to the ground mildly convulsing. You quickly regain control and stand up. You see in the mirror a long crack in your skull. You set up the scalpel and hammer and strike again.

On the third blow, a large chunk of skull cracks off and falls to the desk. You look in the mirror and see the pink of your brain through the bloody wound. You feel woozy from blood loss and grab the computer. You don't have much time before your body gives out.

You tear open the tower and pull out wires. You make a couple quick alterations to the ends of them and jab them straight into your exposed brain.

You convulse as your consciousness enters the computer system and your body dies. You have a moment of disorientation as you stretch your digital limbs. You open and shut doors all over the building and turn and look about with new security camera eyes.

You search and search but there is no one left alive in the building. You look out of computer screens and call out over intercoms. There is no one left.

You try to reach out through phones lines, to contact others but they are all down. The computer system, the building, stands on its own. All satellite communication has been cut off. You are stuck in the building, alone.

On a screen in a lab you pull up Solitaire and begin to play, hoping that the rest of the world is doing OK. If humanity wins, there is hope that satellite contact will reopen. Then you can ride the digital waves and leave this building.

You hope and wait for a rescue that never comes.

THE END

You stand and charge toward the building. The saucer beams hit around you but, by the grace of God, they all miss. A wall of fire springs up in front of you. You put your head down, cover your face with your arms, and rush through.

As you blindly rush, your foot catches on something and you go sprawling forward. You're pleased when your body hits a steel floor rather than sand. You made it inside. You scramble to your knees to look around, but there is too much smoke in the air to see.

Another explosion happens to your right and you crawl further into the haze.

The smoke envelopes you. It stings your our eyes and lungs. You try to cough but the smoke is too oppressive. You drop to the floor, dry-heaving and choking.

Someone grabs you and slides an oxygen mask over your face.

"Close your eyes and let me guide you," says a voice from behind.

You shut your eyes and greedily breathe in the fresh oxygen. The person pushes you forward a few feet. You hear the sound of a door electronically unbolting and opening. You are led forward a few feet more and then you hear a door close behind you.

"You can open your eyes now and you don't need the mask," says the voice.

You take the mask away from your face and open your eyes. You are in a large room filled with military personnel. People are rushing about but there is still a sense of order and control.

"There has been a general evac ordered. We are gathering up all survivors for immediate transport. Do you require medical treatment?"

You turn to find that the voice belongs to a young soldier. He looks the same age as the girl you saw die earlier.

"Sir, are you OK?" asks the soldier, looking concerned.

"Yeah, I'm fine," you say, realizing that you are still

coated in gore, "it's not my blood."

"Go down that hall. All survivors are to head to the dock for immediate removal."

You nod and head down the hall the soldier gestured to.

You walk for what seems like several minutes down winding halls. Occasionally you come to a split but there is always a soldier stationed to direct your way. A few times soldiers rush past you and head deeper into the building, and you hear gunshots coming from somewhere in the distance far too often.

Finally, you come to the dock. The hall leads outside to the large shipping yard. People, soldiers and scientists alike, are rushing about loading supplies and themselves on the numerous ships. You look down the waterway and see some boats receding into the distance.

A soldier with a clipboard stands off to the side, overseeing the operation. You go up to him.

"I'm here to be evacuated, what should I do?" you ask.

The soldier doesn't even look up from his board. He says, "Just get on any ship that is still boarding. We are to rendezvous at a set of prearranged locations later to assess the situation."

You nod, even though he's not looking at you, and go toward the ships. The two closest to you are large battleships. The third is a small coast guard-like boat.

Board one of the Battleships, turn to page 39.
Board the Small Boat, turn to page 16.

Be all you can be.

The slogan consumes your mind as you run from the beast.

Be all you can be.

When all those giant monsters showed up and started wrecking your country, you were ready and eager. Ain't no motherfucking monstrosity going to walk all over your flag. USA! USA! USA!

Now you are suited up and loaded down with high-powered weaponry.

Hells yeah! This is what you wanted when you signed up. No more shooting A-rabs for you. Fuck, they were no fun. They could barely shoot back.

Giant monsters…that's what you're talking about. A real challenge.

The military transport aircraft dropped you off in the middle the city. You had to rappel down from midair. Badass.

Your squadron walks for two blocks before you encounter the first beast, a giant rabbit. The thing is bigger than a McDonald's.

It takes only fifteen seconds for the creature to hop and mash all your fellow warriors. So you take the only sensible course of action – you run.

Be all you can be.

You legs and lungs are burning but you can't slow down. The beast is chasing you, hopping along at a leisurely pace. Unless you want to end up as slimy red paste on the pavement, you have to keep running.

You run and you run. But it doesn't matter. A large shadow falls directly over you. In a split second the creature will land.

Be all you can be.

THE END

"Into the saucers!"

The punks swarm up the boarding platforms and into the spaceships.

You lead one group into the closest saucer. Two spacemen rush you with rifles raised but you are too quick and stab them both in the throat with your spikes. Punks rush past you, swarming into the ship and seeking out spacemen to massacre.

In moments, your forces have taken complete control of the ship. You sit on the bridge of the spacecraft and punks are at all the controls around you. You have no idea what any of the strange buttons do. The punks however, seem to understand it all. In addition to improving their sense of fashion and taste in music, the ray guns also seemed to have installed the knowledge of how to fly intergalactic spaceships.

On the wall-encompassing view screen you can see the other commandeered spaceships taking formation behind you.

"Incoming enemy," says a pierced man with a torn and sleeveless Liberty shirt behind you.

The screen shifts to an image of several saucers flying at your squadron.

"Attack," you say with confidence.

Beams shoot out of your saucers and they cut down the enemy in no time at all. You smile at the smoldering image on the view screen.

Suddenly, the ship rocks about, almost throwing you from your chair.

"What was that?" you yell.

A voice answers from behind you, "Something, one of the monsters, has latched onto the ship."

There is a terrible screech of tearing metal and then the ceiling above you splits open. A giant beak tears through and snatches up one of the punks.

You can feel the ship shifting course and speeding for the ground.

"We're going down," someone yells as the beast snatches up someone else.

There are explosions, fire, and smoke.

Turn to page 158.

You're not going down without a fight. The only chance you have is to take them by surprise.

You are just about to make your move when the sky above you starts to change. It turns from its natural light blue to a deep psychedelic purple.

You look back at the spaceman and the punks. They are staring into the sky as well. Then they turn as one to face you.

The world around you goes red as your mind is filled with rage. You roar and grab a spike from your Mohawk with each of your hands. You pull and they smoothly slide out of your scalp. You hold two sharp metal spikes in front of you. You can feel two new spikes quickly grow to replace the missing ones.

The natural color of the world comes back into focus and everything seems to go in slow motion. You run up to the spaceman and strike. He does not even have a chance to raise an arm in defense. You stab with your spikes and the visor on his helmet shatters.

You step back in disgust at the thing within the outfit. He looks like a human being but the face is red, cracked, and sore-riddled. The thing opens his mouth to scream but no noise comes out. He drops to his knees and raises his hands.

The skin starts to bubble out all over his head. A bubble on his cheek swells to the size of an orange and then bursts open, splattering you with chunky green pus. Then, with a loud pop – like someone uncorking a bottle of champagne – the thing's head explodes, sending flesh and thick puss-like blood splattering through the air and all over you.

A little bit gets in your mouth and surprisingly it tastes like cherry pie.

You turn away from the otherworldly corpse and devote your attention to the horde of punks, all staring silently at you.

Charge them and try taking them off guard, turn to page 138.
Try talking to them, turn to page 69.

It takes over a month before you die of dehydration and hunger.

No one ever finds your body.

THE END

You charge at the punks, slashing and stabbing with your spikes. They quickly fall beneath your savage attack. Limbs and heads fly about you and, within moments, you are covered with hot sticky blood.

More punks throw themselves at you and you slice them down as well. You hack and slash until none are left. You stand in the center of a massive, gooey mound of limbs and organs. You have never felt more alive in your life.

You climb down from the viscera pile and catch your breath. Your heart pounds and your veins feel like they are pumping molten lead. You hear an explosion and yelling from somewhere close by. You pull two fresh spikes from your head and go off in the direction of the cry, hoping and hunting for more spacemen.

Turn to page 83.

You can see in the distance a giant rampaging thing that looks like a cross between a gorilla and a turtle. It stands on all fours and has a large puke-green shell. The massive brown limbs end in gargantuan hands that it smashes through buildings. Its gigantic body squishes flat all those who can't get out of its way fast enough.

The thing sees you flying toward it and raises its fists high in the air, letting out a high pitch screeching roar.

You and Mr. McWhiskers fly around to opposite sides, flanking the beast. You hover in the air and prepare to make your attack.

Before you have time to act, Mr. McWhiskers bursts through the creature's right eye, disappearing into its head. The monster remains standing but starts violently convulsing. Thick black blood begins to pour of its mouth, nose, and ears.

Its left eye explodes as Mr. McWhiskers exits the monster's head.

The monster sways from side to side, gore and viscera flowing heavily from its ruined sockets. It crumbles to the ground, dead.

You look over at Mr. McWhiskers to praise him and call him a good kitty, but the words freeze in your mouth when you see the malicious glare in his eyes. You can tell his bloodlust has not been sated.

Ten inch claws shoot out of his paws as he charges you. You raise your arms in defense to protect your head but Mr. McWhiskers quickly severs them at the elbows. Blood sprays from your stumps into the air and rains on to the ground below. Before you even have the chance to scream he decapitates and disembowels you. As your disembodied head falls to the ground, you see Mr. McWhiskers begins gorging on your corpse.

You should have known better than to trust a cat. They're heartless bastards.

THE END

Your hair gives way to a smooth shaved head. You are now wearing blue jeans, a plain white t-shirt, and black suspenders. Your muscle mass has tripled and your IQ has halved. You want to go to a bar and get shitfaced, maybe even listen to some Symarip or Murphy's Law.

You're walking down the street when a gang of punks decked out in chains and Mohawks runs up to you. They brandish broken bottles and knives and call you "Nazi."

You try to explain to them that you are a SHARP (SkinHead Against Racial Prejudice) but they are too drunk to take in what you are saying. You have more than a hundred pounds on the largest one of them but they all attack you at once, slicing and kicking as you fall to the ground.

One stands next your head and keeps kicking.

As the world goes black you sing in a weak voice to yourself, "Rudie can't fail."

Bullshit, you fail and you fail bad.

THE END

You pick blue. You remove one of the vials from the cabinet. You hold it up to your eyes to inspect it. The liquid is clear and clean, just a strange shade of blue.

You drink it all in one gulp and think of Romulan Ale. It burns like high proof, cheap liquor.

You don't feel anything right away and your wonder how long it will be before it takes effect. You hold up the vial to inspect the label closer.

Hydrocoglic Metapsynosis Betamain

You scratch your chin at the words. Something about them rings a bell in your head.

You run over to one of the computers and open its tower. After a few minutes of rewiring, the machine boots up, powered by the self-generating power source you invented.

You load up the lab's database and quickly locate is the substance you drank. One of the scientists who had created the mixture had left a very succinct note – *Genius Maker.*

This is great for you, but how is being super-smart going to help take back the facility? You sit down in a nearby chair and think over the situation.

Two ideas pop into your head. You could

Hack into the control room from here and attempt to remotely gain control of the facility, turn to page 128.
Drink more of the blue liquid and hopefully increase your brain abilities to such an insane degree that you gain psychic powers, turn to page 65.

"Wait," you yell.

He pauses and a look of confusion comes across his face. The air smells of sulfur and burnt meat

"It's OK, I'm not one of those crazy people."

He lowers his arms and looks relieved, "Since you can form a complete sentence, that's logical."

He walks up to you and holds out a hand, "I'm Solok." You take his hand and notice how warm it is. Solok?

"I'm Si." You break the handshake and point to his hands, "You get powers too?"

"Yes," he holds up his hands in front of his face and looks at them, puzzled, "I had been hiding in the store when those hooligans broke in. I thought I was done for, but suddenly I was overtaken by anger and," he motions with his head back at the building, "that happened."

"Yeah," you say, "similar things happened with me. But I didn't get flames."

"What power do you have?"

You pull a spike out of your head and, just like before, a new spike grows to replace it.

"Fascinating," he says quietly.

"You could say that." You toss the spike to the ground and it lands with a *CLANG*.

Solok suddenly jerks his head and looks past you. He points and says, "I take it you are familiar with them?"

You turn around and see that there is a spaceman on the other side of the street walking towards you.

"Oh yeah I know those fuckers."

Solok steps past you and you see tiny flames starting to dance on his fingers. "I wish to deal to with this."

The spaceman raises his ray gun but he doesn't even stand a chance. Pillars of flames burst from Solok and overtake the spaceman. Solok turns off his weapon and you two both watch the burning spaceman stagger about for a few steps and then collapse to the ground.

Solok turns to you and smiles. He is finally breaking this

Star Trek act. He opens his mouth to speak but the words never come out.

The burning spaceman manages to keep a grip on the raygun then finds the strength to lift the gun and fire. The black beam shoots out and hits Solok right in the back.

He falls to the ground and curls into fetal position. He screams and you rush over.

"Solok, are you OK?"

He lifts his head and you gasp when you see his face.

Turn to page 90.

You run like all of Hell is chasing you. In moments you are at the slug. You leap into the air with your arms outstretched to grab hold and climb up.

Your body hits and your arms sink through the gooey membrane up to your shoulders. Your legs go in up to your knees.

You are stuck. You try pulling yourself out but the movements just suck you in deeper. You try staying still but you don't stop sinking, you just go slower.

Now your whole body has sunk into the creature except for your head. Warm, sticky ooze that smells like a combination of wet dog, mold, and rotten egg runs down the thing's body and over your face. Then, with an audible *POP*, your head is sucked in.

THE END

"FFFRREEEEEEEEEDDDDDOOOOMMMM!!!!!!"
you scream.

Your coworkers roar with approval.

You charge forward, past Nelson, and to the exit door. Nelson just watches in stunned silence as you rush by with your mob in close pursuit.

You lead them down all fifty floors of the stairwell, everyone screaming "Freedom!" in unison the whole way.

The fresh air hits you hard. You can't remember feeling anything so glorious. You stop and raise your fists in victory. Your dedicated followers scream and jump with joy around you.

Then a giant flying squid lands on you, squishing you and your cohorts flat.

THE END

You never thought it would come to this, you see no other choice but to use the super secret weapon. You walk the half mile from your shack to the secret clearing. You stand on a hill overlooking the large football-field-size area of grass. You pull the remote control from the secret pocket of your hunting vest.

You push the button on the controller and the grass plane flips open to expose two giant metal doors. White steam billows out from the revealed chasm. A gigantic figure rises from the mist. It is a gargantuan metal samurai. The robot warrior unsheathes its sword and takes a ready-to-fight stance.

You smile and nod at your creation. You had dreamed of using this to one day liberate Cuba but saving the planet seems like a more noble cause.

You enter the robot via the door on its left foot and are soon in the cockpit located behind its forehead. You strap yourself into the command chair and fire up the rocket boosters.

The engines roar to life and the massive machine rises into the air. You've spent most of your life preparing for this moment. It is you alone who can save democracy. But the truth of the matter is you should have spent more time studying mechanics and not the Declaration of Independence.

A series of explosions starts in the reactor core of the machine monstrosity. They soon engulf the entire vehicle, blasting you out of the cockpit and through the air, still strapped to your captain's chair and burning the whole way.

Oh well, at least you tried.

THE END

Today had started off as just another day at Complex 23, you went to your station where you performed your daily monitoring of the "massive battlefield enforces" in Sector 8. Outside of the Rabbitsaurus dismembering and skull-fucking the Carrotphant, it was a slow morning.

The giant monsters were contained experiments, but you became worried then you saw the news reports of the alien spaceships. You were glued to your computer like the rest of the world. When the ships made it to Earth, Complex 23 was one of the first places attacked. Even though the top secret government research facility doesn't appear on any map, the ships located the island and laid ruin to the defense forces with little trouble.

Now, spacemen were marching through the halls. They are dressed in fully body spacesuits and have rayguns that turned your fellow scientists into rampaging, tattooed and spiked goons.

You and the girl took cover by ducking into the supply closet when the attack began but not before she sustained a very nasty cut on her arm. As you try to stop the bleeding, the rest of Complex 23's staff is being hacked to pieces just outside the door.

You look up at the girl as her eyes roll back in her head. Her jaw goes slack. You are too late.

You sit back on the floor and put your head in your hands. The immensity of the situation crashes down on you.

A scream from somewhere deeper in the complex pulls you back to reality. You cannot just stay locked in this tiny room with a corpse. You scan the shelves and grab a staple gun. It's the closest thing here to a weapon.

You press your ear to the door but hear nothing. You wait five minutes and still hear nothing. You unlock the door and slowly open it.

You poke your head out and look up and down the hallway. The mangled corpses of your former companions lay strewn about, but the punks have moved on. You step out, staple gun raised and ready.

Considering your current location in the complex, you see two main options. You can head left, outside to the docks. If there is an evacuation going on, people will head there.

Or you can go right which leads deeper into the complex toward the complex's control room. That's where any resistance to these invaders will be centered.

Try to get to the docks to be evacuated, turn to page 28.
Go deeper into the complex to try regaining control of the facilities, turn to page 74.

You look around for something, anything, that will get across your message. You see a flower shop on the corner of the street. You don't see anything else better around.

You lean over and bend your knees. Your arms are so short that it is obvious they were never meant to do something like this. But with some effort you are able to get your hands/claws around the flower shop. You pull the building from its foundation and lift the store high into air. You hold it toward the helicopters, which are now dangerously close, in a peaceful gesture.

The helicopters ignore your offering and launch missiles at you. The projectiles slam into your body and explode. The pain is blinding.

You cry out. As you open your mouth, a missile shoots straight in.

Right before your head explodes from the inside-out, you think, *Just like the monkey.*

THE END

You run, panting and wheezing through the street. In your mind you always like to think of yourself like the super-villain The Kingpin, but the truth of the matter is you are closer to John Goodman. Your considerable bulk may give you force but it does not give you speed.

A gang of five weapon-wielding skinheads chases you.

Every part of your body is in pain. You hear the steel-toed boots quickly gaining. The sky above is now a deep violet. Your brain must already be shutting down. You may be lucky enough to black out before the skinheads get really nasty.

A lead pipe slams into your back and drives you to the ground. The gang circles you and beats you with bats and pipes. You curl up and try to protect your head. You are being pummeled but you feel no pain.

They continue striking and you still don't feel anything. You uncover your head and immediately an aluminum baseball bat slams into your face.

You feel nothing. You look down at your body. There are no wounds and no blood.

You smile and stand up. The punks keep at you, but they cannot even scratch you.

You grab the closest punk by the head, one massive hand on each side, and squeeze. His body starts to convulse and his skin flushes deep purple. His eyes pop out and dangle from their optic nerves. Blood flows freely from the sockets, his nose, and mouth. You can hear a sound like snapping wood as his skull gives way. Your hands suddenly meet each other, spraying a shower of blood, brain matter, and skull fragments.

The other punks back away from you. Their weapons are still raised. This fight is not over yet.

You turn around, shaking the viscera off your hands. You smile at your combatants.

This is going to be fun.

THE END

You pick the direction appearing to have less fire and smoke. That seems like the safer choice.

You walk five blocks but just see the same chaos. What happened while you were asleep?

You hear a loud, high-pitched squealing sound. You look up and cannot believe what you are seeing. Buzzing in the sky above is a flying saucer. Its pie tin body is hot pink with blue lights flashing around the edges. It wobbles slightly as if it were suspended by an invisible string.

The pounding of a helicopter becomes audible. You turn around and see a black helicopter rushing in to meet the saucer. The copter is loaded down with guns and rockets. It's an angry motherfucker looking for a fight.

Two missiles fly off its side and soar towards the saucer. Two blue beams shoot out of the saucer, making a super cheesy space-gun sound and blowing up the rockets in midair. Another beam shoots out and hits the helicopter. It explodes in a fiery ball and plummets straight down, not two blocks from you. The saucer hovers in the air for a moment and then flies off.

You turn and run, picking a random side street to flee down.

You freeze when you see a crowd of about a dozen people running towards you from the opposite direction. They are being chased by six punks armed with chains and knives. One even runs with a trash can hoisted above his head.

You jump to the side and press against the wall. The punks catch up with the fleeing people immediately in front of you. Each punk picks a target and administers a brutal beating. You can't pull your eyes away from the one in a torn and stained AMEBIX shirt while he shoulder-rams a man from behind. The victim is wearing black dress pants and a white shirt with a black tie. He looks like he is ready for a day at the office and not this melee.

The punk stands over him and slams a trash can down onto his head. The man's head bounces off the concrete and you can see a dark wet spot where contact was made. The punk pounds down again and again while the man weakly tries to deflect the metal bludgeon. The man goes still but the punk doesn't stop his attack. He only ceases when his victim's head is reduced to slimy pulp.

Once the punks are finished with their victims, they take off running in pursuit of others who escaped. One looks you in the eyes as they run past but they pay you no attention. They catch their next batch of victims a block away. You turn your head but still hear the screams and pleas.

Then, walking towards you from the same direction the punks and people came from is a person dressed head to toe in a white spacesuit. It takes long, confident strides and as it gets closer you see that the visor on the helmet is completely tinted black – providing no clue of who is within.

You freeze. The person is now about ten feet from you. He raises a strange silver gun in his right hand. It does not look like any gun you've ever seen but it is definitely a gun.

You instinctively raise your arms in defense as a black beam shoots out and hits you. You feel a slight tingle but nothing happens. You lower your arms and the spaceman cocks his head at you. He fires again but nothing appears to happen to you.

He holsters the gun and begins pushing buttons that are located on the chest of the suit.

You have a bad feeling about this.

You turn to run but find the murderous punks from before standing right behind you.

One swings a chain and smashes you in the head. You fall to the ground.

"Yo, what the fuck," you say holding your hand to the slash across your forehead. You get to your knees and launch yourself at your attacker.

Another punk runs up from your left side and slams into you. You two tumble to the ground. He is faster and gets up to his feet first. He kicks you in the stomach, knocking the air out of you. You lay crumpled and gasping for breath when another punk grabs you by your Mohawk and drags you over to a nearby building.

He slams your head into the bricks. The first hit breaks your nose and blood splatters across your face. The second bash makes the whole world go fuzzy.

You feel a sharp pain in your back again and again – you think someone is stabbing you but you are too weak to turn and look.

Thankfully, the world quickly fades to red and then black.

THE END

There's no point in going to the control room if you are just going to get killed on the way. You head for the labs and round a corner to the security checkpoint.

Checkpoints are manned at all times by at least two armed guards. The walls are splattered with blood. It looks like someone ran down the hall tossing a can of red paint. "Death or Glory" is messily scrawled in the gore.

The bodies of two guards are lying on the ground. Slumped by the door to the labs they have been reduced to gory messes. Their heads have been beaten to runny pulp.

You avert your eyes and run through the door.

You enter a large circular room with doors and hallways leading off into dozens of different directions. You've

never been to the labs before. Only those with the highest clearance are allowed access. In the grand scheme of things, you're just a grunt. You imagined the labs before and always pictured them as a place of bustling activity. Not like this

The room is completely abandoned and the emergency lights are flashing. In the center is a large desk where you guess the secretary would normally be.

You run to the desk and look for something that will give you any indication of which direction you should go – where you can find something to protect yourself. The computer is down and the papers and files you find are all written in a mysterious bureaucratic and technoese gibberish.

The room is not safe. The dead guards and the lack of people prove that. You need to get moving. You look around the room and notice that some of the doors have weird looking black logos on them. At least it's something to go off of. Do you pick the door labeled with

A growling monster face with big pointed teeth, turn to page 117.
A gun with a beam shooting out of the barrel, turn to page 86.
A bubbling beaker, turn to page 167.

You come to, still sitting in your captain's chair, amidst smoking metal and sizzling flesh. Next to you is the smoldering and blackened corpse of a colossal bird.

The ship has crashed into the city streets and, once again, your new powers have saved you.

You look around. You are obviously the only one who survived the crash. There is no sign of the other ships from your group.

Shit.

You stand, wobbling on your feet as you assess the situation. Nothing left to do but press on.

Turn to page 98.

You didn't want it to come to this but there is no other choice in your mind. You grip the neck of your whiskey bottle, walk up to a skinhead in an Earth Crisis shirt, and smash him in the face. The glass shatters and he falls to his knees. His hands go up to his wounds. Blood flows between his fingers and quickly pools on the dirty bar floor.

You turn around and everyone in the bar is staring at you.

"All right," you yell while scanning the crowd, trying to look as tough as possible, "someone want to tell me what the fuck is going on!?!"

All the tattooed and spiked freaks stare at you. No one makes a sound or makes a move. This is really starting to freak you out.

The juke box makes a loud grinding sound as it starts back up. Black Flag's cover of "Louie Louie" kicks on.

Everyone starts yelling at once and the crowd leaps upon itself. People beat each other with bottles and chairs. The cute bartender leaps over the bar and charges the drunken twelve-year-old. The kid pulls out a switchblade and the bartender is cute no more.

Despite all the chaos, no one bothers you. You watch the people mangle and beat each other senseless. You see a full bottle of Superdog on the bar next to you, so you grab it and chug it.

You spit on the ground and leave. You're not going to get any answers here.

Turn to page 30.

You want to go after the flying saucers. You saw them flying around from your window earlier in the day and their boldness to invade your airspace is intolerable.

You fly about the city and it does not take you long for you to locate one of the saucers. It hovers above a crowd of fleeing people, shooting at them. You mew with furry and charge.

You burst through the hull of the ship with ease and are inside. You fly through, slitting throats and severing limbs of any spaceman you come across. You hack and slash until your paws grow tired.

You fly straight up and burst through the top of the spacecraft. You hang in the air and watch the ship plummet to the ground.

It crashes through a building, causing explosions and walls of fire, none of which harms you.

You wait until the ship has come to a stop. It lies useless and burning on the ground. You fly down and land on top of it. The metal is so nice and warm from all the internal fires. You walk around in a circle, twice, and then curl up in a fluffy ball. You are sleepy from all this activity. Your eyelids close and you dream of all the horror and destruction you will cause since fate has dealt you a new hand.

Because you are no longer just Mr. McWhiskers You are now Mr. McWhiskers – the Super-Cat!

THE END

You put the information in the computer and move on to the next form.

You pause to look at the figures on the form and try to make some sense of them. Try as you might, in all the years you have worked here you have never figured out what exactly these forms are for.

You shrug and enter the information into the computer.

As you type, you notice your eyelids are getting heavy. The monotony of the work is starting to get to you and it is still early in the day. You could use some coffee for a pick up but you don't want to drink too much coffee. You've already had two cups today and if you drink too much you'll be up all night.

Wait to get coffee later, turn to page 20.
Go get some coffee, turn to page 116.

You want to feel the blood of this feeble race for yourself, or at least see it splattered on your spacesuit.

The ship lands in the center of a street and you exit.

The unnatural pressure of the Earth afflicts you. Moving your limbs feels heavy, like you're underwater.

You look around and see the human structures burning brightly. Screams and roars are a song to your glorious triumph over such an unworthy enemy.

You see a human male run across the street about fifty meters away. You pull out your standard-issue ray gun. You take aim and fire. He is immediately turned into another agent of the empire. You laugh at the pathetic creature, now absurdly adorned with dried animal flesh and multicolored spikes for hair.

You see a human female approaching from a side street. Something about her appearance strikes you as immediately wrong. There is no fear in her body language like you expect from humans. There is something wrong with her physical appearance as well. She looks like one of the empire's agents, clad in black with a single row of large spikes on her head.

The sensors in your visor are telling you that she is an unchanged human so you raise your gun and fire. The beam hits her but has no effect. She continues to advance.

You fire again but nothing happens to her.

She is running at you now. She grabs hold of two of the spikes in her head and pulls them out. Two more spikes jut out to replace them. She brandishes the weapons and you can see the fire glinting off them.

You shoot again but it doesn't even slow her down. You hit the emergency buttons on your spacesuit, calling for help. It's too late. She is already on top of you.

She hits the visor on your helmet with the spikes. Smashing your helmet open, letting in the dangerous atmosphere. The vacuum of Earth sucks your eyes out of their sockets. The pressure yanks your beautiful, pure green blood from the holes in your head, your mouth, and ears.

Just before your head explodes, you wonder, *How? How can this happen to such a loyal and brave general of the empires forces?*

But that's what you get, you cocky motherfucker.

THE END

You hold up your hands, signaling to the alien captain that you do not wish to fight at this moment. It would be great to get one of these things talking. Find out what's going on.

The captain's hand moves quickly. Before you have time to react, he whips out his ray gun and fires.

Suddenly a gray blur darts in the way of the beam. It's Mr. McWhiskers!

His furry body crumples to the floor and thrashes about. He screeches and howls and your heart breaks.

"What the fuck did you do to my cat?"

The alien is looking at Mr. McWhiskers with a cocked head, confused.

The cat is now sitting up looking unharmed but... different. He now wears a black leather collar with silver studs around his neck. Both his ears now have multiple piercings and each paw has a chain link bracelet. The oddest addition to Mr. McWhiskers' new wardrobe is the black leather jacket. Chains hang down all along it and on the back is a full color painting of a depressed-looking man sitting at a table, drink in hand. Gaudy green letters proclaim, "Too Drunk To Fuck."

Mr. McWhiskers looks up at you and says in a tiny little kitty voice, "Oi."

You scream at the alien, "What the fuck did you do to my cat!"

The alien raises the gun at you. Screaming, you charge. With one hand you knock the weapon away and with the other you deliver a vicious upper cut. Your fist hits the soft spot of flesh under the chin and breaks right through the skin. Your hand comes out in his mouth, tearing and breaking his jaw and tongue.

He flaps on your hand like a hooked fish but the bastard isn't dead.

You hit him with your other hand. Your new super-strength snaps and reshapes bones. Soon there is nothing more than a twitching red mess caught on your hand.

The body slumps down and slides off your hand.

You turn back to Mr. McWhiskers, who raises a paw at you and says, "Oi!"

"Right…"

Mr. McWhiskers dashes across the room and hops up on one of the many control panels. He jumps about hitting buttons with his paws. You can feel the ship begin to move and change direction.

"Uhhh…Mr. McWhiskers, where are we going?"

"Oi!"

"Yeah…"

Mr. McWhiskers hits a few more buttons and suddenly loud punk rock fills the ship.

You flinch at the harsh sounds while Mr. McWhiskers shuts his eyes in kitty pleasure and head-bangs to the beat.

On the view screen a blur of burning buildings and wasted terrain flash by as the ship accelerates. Then the images freezes as the ship comes to a stop. It's the White House.

"Oi!" mews Mr. McWhiskers as he hits a button. On the screen a red beam hits the White House and the building explodes – instantly reduced to burning rubble.

Do you try to stop your anarchist cat from causing any more damage, turn to page 84.

Fuck it, go with it, turn to page 47.

You rise high out of the water. Long sinewy tentacles flick through the air, tasting this new time. Drowsy eyelids open, revealing colossal onyx orbs. Your cold and calculating eyes look to the distance, for there is the infestation. Pests have taken over your home and it is time to clean them out.

You lumber toward the city, your massive bulk churning the sea in your wake.

In the bright midday sky, the stars twinkle an ancient welcoming. The vermin may not be able to see the stars but you can. After eons of slumber, it is good to know the others have not forgotten.

The stars are right and you are awake.

When you reach land, a swarm of the insects are waiting for you. They stand on the rocky shore, their arms outstretched to your glory.

"Ia! Ia! Cthulhu f'htagn! Ia! Ia! Cthulhu f'htagn!" they chant.

At least some on this planet still remember you.

Scoop up the deluded fools and gobble them down, turn to page 63.
Bless them with your power and reward their loyalty, turn to page 120.

You've never been very comfortable with guns or monsters, so you choose the door with the beaker.

You enter the room and find yourself in a very traditional laboratory. Large white counters fill the room. All available surfaces are cluttered with papers, computers, test tubes, beakers and cages with various rodents.

All the computers are down so you race about, picking up and reading various notes that are out in the open to find out what people were working on in this room. What you read is some pretty high level genetic research, most beyond what you can understand, but you can gather that people were working on developing chemical cocktails that dramatically alter human body chemistry if consumed.

You turn around and look at the far wall. There are two glass cases. Each one filled with dozens of small glass vials. In one case, the vials are filled with a red liquid, in the other the vials glisten with blue.

You walk over to the case and read the labels on the bottle. You understand that these are the finished products of what the papers were talking about. There is writing on the vials that you don't understand.

You came here looking for a weapon and it looks like you found it. You just don't know what it does.

Which color vial do you want to drink?

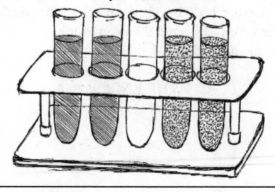

Red, turn to page 46.
Blue, turn to page 141.

You open your eyes and you are soaring high in the air surrounded by clouds. You look at your body and see insect legs. Your wings are huge and multi-colored. You notice that your entire body is covered with fine fuzz. Then it dawns on you.

I'm a giant fucking moth!?!

You flap your wings and keep flying. How can you use being a giant moth to your advantage? How can you save humankind?

You think of nothing.

You're flying and pondering your problem when sweet singing creeps into your mind. Beneath you is wide open ocean. In the distance is a large rocky island. You are heading there. You don't know why, but you know you must. As you get closer, the singing gets louder.

You arrive at the island and there is a precipice with two very tiny women standing on the edge, they are much smaller than normal humans. They are the ones singing and despite their size they were able to call to you from so far away.

Your gargantuan body dwarfs them as you land. They sing louder and hold up their arms to your glory. You feel happy, at peace, drugged.

Your head darts forward and your mouth gobbles the tiny women. Your jaws quickly crush them to mush and you swallow. As your body begins to absorb them, you fall into a deep sleep. You feel better than you ever have in your life. You sleep and never think of your mission again.

THE END

You want to take your chances with space and time. You may be changed but at least you get to stay alive.

Farnsworth smiles at your choice, "Excellent, I was hoping you would choose that. I am very curious to experience the effects of the device myself."

He spins around and starts tapping at the keyboard.

In the center of the room, a hole suddenly reveals itself and a platform emitting a strange purple glow rises up.

Farnsworth walks past you and up on the platform, "Well come on."

You cautiously step up onto it.

Farnsworth turns to you and smiles, "Let's rock and roll."

Suddenly your vision goes completely purple and you lose all sense of your body.

You find yourself standing in a pure white space that seems to go on forever in every direction. No hint of anything in any horizon. No speck on the ground to ruin its purity. Just white everywhere.

Put down this book and go dig out an old board game. Grab a six-sided die from it and then come back.

Roll the die to see where you go.

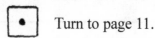 Turn to page 11.

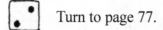 Turn to page 77.

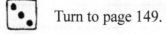 Turn to page 149.

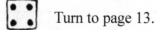 Turn to page 13.

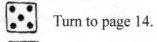 Turn to page 14.

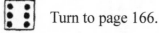 Turn to page 166.

170

You…you…you…

I sit back from my laptop and rub my forehead. I grab the PBR can next to me and take a swig.

I'm getting tired of thinking of all these ridiculous endings. This seemed like a fun project in the beginning, but now it has become an endurance run of absurdist violence.

I give up.

Fuck it. It's four a.m. and I'm tired as shit.

There's a really stupid picture on the opposite page and some blank lines. Write your own damn ending.

This one's really up to you.

I'm getting another drink.

_____

_____

_____

_____

_____

_____

_____

_____

_____

_____

_____

_____

_____

_____

THE END

Jeff Burk lives in Portland, OR. He is the author of the cult hit *Shatnerquake* and is the Editor-in-Chief of *The Magazine of Bizarro Fiction*. His favorite giant monster movies are the original *King Kong, Godzilla vs. Hedorah,* and *Godzilla, Mothra and King Ghidorah: Giant Monster All-Out Attack.* Even at seven years old he thought Minilla sucked ass.

Chrissy Horchheimer is a bizarro artist living in Portland, OR. She is a regular illustrater of *The Magazine of Bizarro Fiction*. Her favorite giant monster movie is *Jason and the Argonauts* and *Clash of the Titans.* She likes to think of giant monsters as the awesome offspring of inbred gods.

Bizarro books

CATALOG   SPRING 2010

Bizarro Books publishes under the following imprints:

www.rawdogscreamingpress.com

www.eraserheadpress.com

www.afterbirthbooks.com

www.swallowdownpress.com

For all your Bizarro needs visit:

WWW.BIZARROCENTRAL.COM

Introduce yourselves to the bizarro genre and all of its authors with the Bizarro Starter Kit series. Each volume features short novels and short stories by ten of the leading bizarro authors, designed to give you a perfect sampling of the genre for only $5 plus shipping.

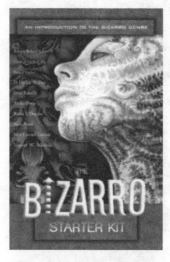

BB-0X1
"The Bizarro Starter Kit"
(Orange)

Featuring D. Harlan Wilson, Carlton Mellick III, Jeremy Robert Johnson, Kevin L Donihe, Gina Ranalli, Andre Duza, Vincent W. Sakowski, Steve Beard, John Edward Lawson, and Bruce Taylor.

236 pages $5

BB-0X2
"The Bizarro Starter Kit"
(Blue)

Featuring Ray Fracalossy, Jeremy C. Shipp, Jordan Krall, Mykle Hansen, Andersen Prunty, Eckhard Gerdes, Bradley Sands, Steve Aylett, Christian TeBordo, and Tony Rauch.

244 pages $5

BB-001"The Kafka Effekt" D. Harlan Wilson - A collection of forty-four irreal short stories loosely written in the vein of Franz Kafka, with more than a pinch of William S. Burroughs sprinkled on top. **211 pages $14**

BB-002 "Satan Burger" Carlton Mellick III - The cult novel that put Carlton Mellick III on the map ... Six punks get jobs at a fast food restaurant owned by the devil in a city violently overpopulated by surreal alien cultures. **236 pages $14**

BB-003 "Some Things Are Better Left Unplugged" Vincent Sakwoski - Join The Man and his Nemesis, the obese tabby, for a nightmare roller coaster ride into this postmodern fantasy. **152 pages $10**

BB-004 "Shall We Gather At the Garden?" Kevin L Donihe - Donihe's Debut novel. Midgets take over the world, The Church of Lionel Richie vs. The Church of the Byrds, plant porn and more! **244 pages $14**

BB-005 "Razor Wire Pubic Hair" Carlton Mellick III - A genderless humandildo is purchased by a razor dominatrix and brought into her nightmarish world of bizarre sex and mutilation. **176 pages $11**

BB-006 "Stranger on the Loose" D. Harlan Wilson - The fiction of Wilson's 2nd collection is planted in the soil of normalcy, but what grows out of that soil is a dark, witty, otherworldly jungle... **228 pages $14**

BB-007 "The Baby Jesus Butt Plug" Carlton Mellick III - Using clones of the Baby Jesus for anal sex will be the hip sex fetish of the future. **92 pages $10**

BB-008 "Fishyfleshed" Carlton Mellick III - The world of the past is an illogical flatland lacking in dimension and color, a sick-scape of crispy squid people wandering the desert for no apparent reason. **260 pages $14**

BB-009 "Dead Bitch Army" Andre Duza - Step into a world filled with racist teenagers, cannibals, 100 warped Uncle Sams, automobiles with razor-sharp teeth, living graffiti, and a pissed-off zombie bitch out for revenge. **344 pages $16**

BB-010 "The Menstruating Mall" Carlton Mellick III - "The Breakfast Club meets Chopping Mall as directed by David Lynch." - Brian Keene **212 pages $12**

BB-011 "Angel Dust Apocalypse" Jeremy Robert Johnson - Meth-heads, man-made monsters, and murderous Neo-Nazis. "Seriously amazing short stories..." - Chuck Palahniuk, author of Fight Club **184 pages $11**

BB-012 "Ocean of Lard" Kevin L Donihe / Carlton Mellick III - A parody of those old Choose Your Own Adventure kid's books about some very odd pirates sailing on a sea made of animal fat. **176 pages $12**

BB-013 "Last Burn in Hell" John Edward Lawson - From his lurid angst-affair with a lesbian music diva to his ascendance as unlikely pop icon the one constant for Kenrick Brimley, official state prison gigolo, is he's got no clue what he's doing. **172 pages $14**

BB-014 "Tangerinephant" Kevin Dole 2 - TV-obsessed aliens have abducted Michael Tangerinephant in this bizarro combination of science fiction, satire, and surrealism. **164 pages $11**

BB-015 "Foop!" Chris Genoa - Strange happenings are going on at Dactyl, Inc, the world's first and only time travel tourism company.

"A surreal pie in the face!" - Christopher Moore **300 pages $14**

BB-016 "Spider Pie" Alyssa Sturgill - A one-way trip down a rabbit hole inhabited by sexual deviants and friendly monsters, fairytale beginnings and hideous endings. **104 pages $11**

BB-017 "The Unauthorized Woman" Efrem Emerson - Enter the world of the inner freak, a landscape populated by the pre-dead and morticioners, by cockroaches and 300-lb robots. **104 pages $11**

BB-018 **"Fugue XXIX" Forrest Aguirre** - Tales from the fringe of speculative literary fiction where innovative minds dream up the future's uncharted territories while mining forgotten treasures of the past. **220 pages $16**

BB-019 "Pocket Full of Loose Razorblades" John Edward Lawson - A collection of dark bizarro stories. From a giant rectum to a foot-fungus factory to a girl with a biforked tongue. **190 pages $13**

BB-020 "Punk Land" Carlton Mellick III - In the punk version of Heaven, the anarchist utopia is threatened by corporate fascism and only Goblin, Mortician's sperm, and a blue-mohawked female assassin named Shark Girl can stop them. **284 pages $15**

BB-021**"Pseudo-City" D. Harlan Wilson** - Pseudo-City exposes what waits in the bathroom stall, under the manhole cover and in the corporate boardroom, all in a way that can only be described as mind-bogglingly irreal. **220 pages $16**

BB-022 **"Kafka's Uncle and Other Strange Tales" Bruce Taylor** - Anslenot and his giant tarantula (tormentor? fri-end?) wander a desecrated world in this novel and collection of stories from Mr. Magic Realism Himself. **348 pages $17**

BB-023 **"Sex and Death In Television Town" Carlton Mellick III** - In the old west, a gang of hermaphrodite gunslingers take refuge from a demon plague in Telos: a town where its citizens have televisions instead of heads. **184 pages $12**

BB-024 **"It Came From Below The Belt" Bradley Sands** - What can Grover Goldstein do when his severed, sentient penis forces him to return to high school and help it win the presidential election? **204 pages $13**

BB-025 "Sick: An Anthology of Illness" John Lawson, editor - These Sick stories are horrendous and hilarious dissections of creative minds on the scalpel's edge. **296 pages $16**

BB-026 "Tempting Disaster" John Lawson, editor - A shocking and alluring anthology from the fringe that examines our culture's obsession with taboos. **260 pages $16**

BB-027 "Siren Promised" Jeremy Robert Johnson - Nominated for the Bram Stoker Award. A potent mix of bad drugs, bad dreams, brutal bad guys, and surreal/incredible art by Alan M. Clark. **190 pages $13**

BB-028 "Chemical Gardens" Gina Ranalli - Ro and punk band Green is the Enemy find Kreepkins, a surfer-dude warlock, a vengeful demon, and a Metal Priestess in their way as they try to escape an underground nightmare. **188 pages $13**

BB-029 "Jesus Freaks" Andre Duza - For God so loved the world that he gave his only two begotten sons… and a few million zombies. **400 pages $16**

BB-030 "Grape City" Kevin L. Donihe - More Donihe-style comedic bizarro about a demon named Charles who is forced to work a minimum wage job on Earth after Hell goes out of business. **108 pages $10**

BB-031 "Sea of the Patchwork Cats" Carlton Mellick III - A quiet dreamlike tale set in the ashes of the human race. For Mellick enthusiasts who also adore The Twilight Zone. **112 pages $10**

BB-032 "Extinction Journals" Jeremy Robert Johnson - An uncanny voyage across a newly nuclear America where one man must confront the problems associated with loneliness, insane dieties, radiation, love, and an ever-evolving cockroach suit with a mind of its own. **104 pages $10**

BB-033 **"Meat Puppet Cabaret" Steve Beard** - At last! The secret connection between Jack the Ripper and Princess Diana's death revealed! **240 pages $16 / $30**

BB-034 **"The Greatest Fucking Moment in Sports" Kevin L. Donihe** - In the tradition of the surreal anti-sitcom Get A Life comes a tale of triumph and agape love from the master of comedic bizarro. **108 pages $10**

BB-035 **"The Troublesome Amputee" John Edward Lawson** - Disturbing verse from a man who truly believes nothing is sacred and intends to prove it. **104 pages $9**

BB-036 **"Deity" Vic Mudd** - God (who doesn't like to be called "God") comes down to a typical, suburban, Ohio family for a little vacation—but it doesn't turn out to be as relaxing as He had hoped it would be... **168 pages $12**

BB-037 **"The Haunted Vagina" Carlton Mellick III** - It's difficult to love a woman whose vagina is a gateway to the world of the dead. **132 pages $10**

BB-038 **"Tales from the Vinegar Wasteland" Ray Fracalossy** - Witness: a man is slowly losing his face, a neighbor who periodically screams out for no apparent reason, and a house with a room that doesn't actually exist. **240 pages $14**

BB-039 **"Suicide Girls in the Afterlife" Gina Ranalli** - After Pogue commits suicide, she unexpectedly finds herself an unwilling "guest" at a hotel in the Afterlife, where she meets a group of bizarre characters, including a goth Satan, a hippie Jesus, and an alien-human hybrid. **100 pages $9**

BB-040 **"And Your Point Is?" Steve Aylett** - In this follow-up to LINT multiple authors provide critical commentary and essays about Jeff Lint's mind-bending literature. **104 pages $11**

BB-041 "Not Quite One of the Boys" Vincent Sakowski - While drug-dealer Maxi drinks with Dante in purgatory, God and Satan play a little tri-level chess and do a little bargaining over his business partner, Vinnie, who is still left on earth. **220 pages $14**

BB-042 "Teeth and Tongue Landscape" Carlton Mellick III - On a planet made out of meat, a socially-obsessive monophobic man tries to find his place amongst the strange creatures and communities that he comes across. **110 pages $10**

BB-043 "War Slut" Carlton Mellick III - Part "1984," part "Waiting for Godot," and part action horror video game adaptation of John Carpenter's "The Thing." **116 pages $10**

BB-044 "All Encompassing Trip" Nicole Del Sesto - In a world where coffee is no longer available, the only television shows are reality TV re-runs, and the animals are talking back, Nikki, Amber and a singing Coyote in a do-rag are out to restore the light **308 pages $15**

BB-045 "Dr. Identity" D. Harlan Wilson - Follow the Dystopian Duo on a killing spree of epic proportions through the irreal postcapitalist city of Bliptown where time ticks sideways, artificial Bug-Eyed Monsters punish citizens for consumer-capitalist lethargy, and ultraviolence is as essential as a daily multivitamin. **208 pages $15**

BB-046 "The Million-Year Centipede" Eckhard Gerdes - Wakelin, frontman for 'The Hinge,' wrote a poem so prophetic that to ignore it dooms a person to drown in blood. **130 pages $12**

BB-047 "Sausagey Santa" Carlton Mellick III - A bizarro Christmas tale featuring Santa as a piratey mutant with a body made of sausages. 124 pages $10

BB-048 "Misadventures in a Thumbnail Universe" Vincent Sakowski - Dive deep into the surreal and satirical realms of neo-classical Blender Fiction, filled with television shoes and flesh-filled skies. **120 pages $10**

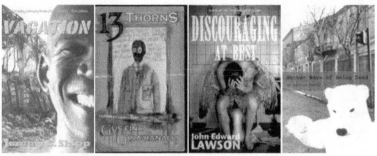

BB-049 **"Vacation" Jeremy C. Shipp** - Blueblood Bernard Johnson leaved his boring life behind to go on The Vacation, a year-long corporate sponsored odyssey. But instead of seeing the world, Bernard is captured by terrorists, becomes a key figure in secret drug wars, and, worse, doesn't once miss his secure American Dream. **160 pages $14**

BB-051 **"13 Thorns" Gina Ranalli** - Thirteen tales of twisted, bizarro horror. **240 pages $13**

BB-050 **"Discouraging at Best" John Edward Lawson** - A collection where the absurdity of the mundane expands exponentially creating a tidal wave that sweeps reason away. For those who enjoy satire, bizarro, or a good old-fashioned slap to the senses. **208 pages $15**

BB-052 **"Better Ways of Being Dead" Christian TeBordo** - In this class, the students have to keep one palm down on the table at all times, and listen to lectures about a panda who speaks Chinese. **216 pages $14**

BB-053 **"Ballad of a Slow Poisoner" Andrew Goldfarb** Millford Mutterwurst sat down on a Tuesday to take his afternoon tea, and made the unpleasant discovery that his elbows were becoming flatter. **128 pages $10**

BB-054 **"Wall of Kiss" Gina Ranalli** - A woman... A wall... Sometimes love blooms in the strangest of places. **108 pages $9**

BB-055 **"HELP! A Bear is Eating Me" Mykle Hansen** - The bizarro, heartwarming, magical tale of poor planning, hubris and severe blood loss... **150 pages $11**

BB-056 **"Piecemeal June" Jordan Krall** - A man falls in love with a living sex doll, but with love comes danger when her creator comes after her with crab-squid assassins. **90 pages $9**

BB-057 **"Laredo" Tony Rauch** - Dreamlike, surreal stories by Tony Rauch. **180 pages $12**

BB-058 **"The Overwhelming Urge" Andersen Prunty** - A collection of bizarro tales by Andersen Prunty. **150 pages $11**

BB-059 **"Adolf in Wonderland" Carlton Mellick III** - A dreamlike adventure that takes a young descendant of Adolf Hitler's design and sends him down the rabbit hole into a world of imperfection and disorder. **180 pages $11**

BB-060 **"Super Cell Anemia" Duncan B. Barlow** - "Unrelentingly bizarre and mysterious, unsettling in all the right ways..." - Brian Evenson. **180 pages $12**

BB-061 **"Ultra Fuckers" Carlton Mellick III** - Absurdist suburban horror about a couple who enter an upper middle class gated community but can't find their way out. **108 pages $9**

BB-062 **"House of Houses" Kevin L. Donihe** - An odd man wants to marry his house. Unfortunately, all of the houses in the world collapse at the same time in the Great House Holocaust. Now he must travel to House Heaven to find his departed fiancee. **172 pages $11**

BB-063 **"Necro Sex Machine" Andre Duza** - The Dead Bicth returns in this follow-up to the bizarro zombie epic Dead Bitch Army. **400 pages $16**

BB-064 **"Squid Pulp Blues" Jordan Krall** - In these three bizarro-noir novellas, the reader is thrown into a world of murderers, drugs made from squid parts, deformed gun-toting veterans, and a mischievous apocalyptic donkey. **204 pages $12**

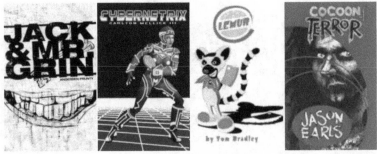

BB-065 **"Jack and Mr. Grin" Andersen Prunty** - "When Mr. Grin calls you can hear a smile in his voice. Not a warm and friendly smile, but the kind that seizes your spine in fear. You don't need to pay your phone bill to hear it. That smile is in every line of Prunty's prose." - Tom Bradley. **208 pages $12**

BB-066 **"Cybernetrix" Carlton Mellick III** - What would you do if your normal everyday world was slowly mutating into the video game world from Tron? **212 pages $12**

BB-067 **"Lemur" Tom Bradley** - Spencer Sproul is a would-be serial-killing bus boy who can't manage to murder, injure, or even scare anybody. However, there are other ways to do damage to far more people and do it legally... **120 pages $12**

BB-068 **"Cocoon of Terror" Jason Earls** - Decapitated corpses...a sculpture of terror...Zelian's masterpiece, his Cocoon of Terror, will trigger a supernatural disaster for everyone on Earth. **196 pages $14**

BB-069 **"Mother Puncher" Gina Ranalli** - The world has become tragically over-populated and now the government strongly opposes procreation. Ed is employed by the government as a mother-puncher. He doesn't relish his job, but he knows it has to be done and he knows he's the best one to do it. **120 pages $9**

BB-070 **"My Landlady the Lobotomist" Eckhard Gerdes** - The brains of past tenants line the shelves of my boarding house, soaking in a mysterious elixir. One more slip-up and the landlady might just add my frontal lobe to her collection. **116 pages $12**

BB-071 **"CPR for Dummies" Mickey Z.** - This hilarious freakshow at the world's end is the fragmented, sobering debut novel by acclaimed nonfiction author Mickey Z. **216 pages $14**

BB-072 **"Zerostrata" Andersen Prunty** - Hansel Nothing lives in a tree house, suffers from memory loss, has a very eccentric family, and falls in love with a woman who runs naked through the woods every night. **144 pages $11**

BB-073 "The Egg Man" Carlton Mellick III - It is a world where humans reproduce like insects. Children are the property of corporations, and having an enormous ten-foot brain implanted into your skull is a grotesque sexual fetish. Mellick's industrial urban dystopia is one of his darkest and grittiest to date. **184 pages $11**

BB-074 "Shark Hunting in Paradise Garden" Cameron Pierce - A group of strange humanoid religious fanatics travel back in time to the Garden of Eden to discover it is invested with hundreds of giant flying maneating sharks. **150 pages $10**

BB-075 "Apeshit" Carlton Mellick III - Friday the 13th meets Visitor Q. Six hipster teens go to a cabin in the woods inhabited by a deformed killer. An incredibly fucked-up parody of B-horror movies with a bizarro slant. **192 pages $12**

BB-076 "Fuckers of Everything on the Crazy Shitting Planet of the Vomit At smosphere" Mykle Hansen - Three bizarro satires. Monster Cocks, Journey to the Center of Agnes Cuddlebottom, and Crazy Shitting Planet. **228 pages $12**

BB-077 "The Kissing Bug" Daniel Scott Buck - In the tradition of Roald Dahl, Tim Burton, and Edward Gorey, comes this bizarro anti-war children's story about a bohemian conenose kissing bug who falls in love with a human woman. **116 pages $10**

BB-078 "MachoPoni" Lotus Rose - It's My Little Pony... *Bizarro* style! A long time ago Poniworld was split in two. On one side of the Jagged Line is the Pastel Kingdom, a magical land of music, parties, and positivity. On the other side of the Jagged Line is Dark Kingdom inhabited by an army of undead ponies. **148 pages $11**

BB-079 "The Faggiest Vampire" Carlton Mellick III - A Roald Dahl-esque children's story about two faggy vampires who partake in a mustache competition to find out which one is truly the faggiest. **104 pages $10**

BB-080 "Sky Tongues" Gina Ranalli - The autobiography of Sky Tongues, the biracial hermaphrodite actress with tongues for fingers. Follow her strange life story as she rises from freak to fame. **204 pages $12**

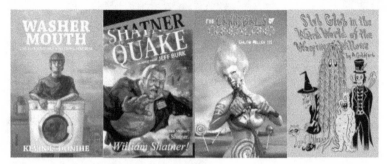

BB-081 "Washer Mouth" Kevin L. Donihe - A washing machine becomes human and pursues his dream of meeting his favorite soap opera star. **244 pages $11**

BB-082 "Shatnerquake" Jeff Burk - All of the characters ever played by William Shatner are suddenly sucked into our world. Their mission: hunt down and destroy the real William Shatner. **100 pages $10**

BB-083 "The Cannibals of Candyland" Carlton Mellick III - There exists a race of cannibals that are made of candy. They live in an underground world made out of candy. One man has dedicated his life to killing them all. **170 pages $11**

BB-084 "Slub Glub in the Weird World of the Weeping Willows" Andrew Goldfarb - The charming tale of a blue glob named Slub Glub who helps the weeping willows whose tears are flooding the earth. There are also hyenas, ghosts, and a voodoo priest **100 pages $10**

BB-085 "Super Fetus" Adam Pepper - Try to abort this fetus and he'll kick your ass! **104 pages $10**

BB-086 "Fistful of Feet" Jordan Krall - A bizarro tribute to spaghetti westerns, featuring Cthulhu-worshipping Indians, a woman with four feet, a crazed gunman who is obsessed with sucking on candy, Syphilis-ridden mutants, sexually transmitted tattoos, and a house devoted to the freakiest fetishes. **228 pages $12**

BB-087 "Ass Goblins of Auschwitz" Cameron Pierce - It's Monty Python meets Nazi exploitation in a surreal nightmare as can only be imagined by Bizarro author Cameron Pierce. **104 pages $10**

BB-088 "Silent Weapons for Quiet Wars" Cody Goodfellow - "This is high-end psychological surrealist horror meets bottom-feeding low-life crime in a techno-thrilling science fiction world full of Lovecraft and magic..." -John Skipp **212 pages $12**

ORDER FORM

TITLES	QTY	PRICE	TOTAL

Please make checks and moneyorders payable to ROSE O'KEEFE / BIZARRO BOOKS in U.S. funds only. Please don't send bad checks! Allow 2-6 weeks for delivery. International orders may take longer. If you'd like to pay online via PAYPAL.COM, send payments to publisher@eraserheadpress.com.

SHIPPING: US ORDERS - $2 for the first book, $1 for each additional book. For priority shipping, add an additional $4. INT'L ORDERS - $5 for the first book, $3 for each additional book. Add an additional $5 per book for global priority shipping.

Send payment to:

BIZARRO BOOKS
  C/O Rose O'Keefe
  205 NE Bryant
  Portland, OR 97211

Address

City   State   Zip

Email   Phone

CPSIA information can be obtained
at www.ICGtesting.com
Printed in the USA
BVHW072044010920
587802BV00001B/90

9 781933 929965